The Hawk

A Midwinter Sellsword

Gladiators & Thieves

Ashes to Ashes

Joshua Robertson

CRIMSON
EDGE
PRESS

Dedication

To those who cross their fingers and hope to fly.

Table of Contents

Thrice Nine Legends Saga

ANAERFELL*

The Kaelandur Series
MELKORKA*
DYNDAER*
MAHARIA**

The Hawkhurst Saga

A MIDWINTER SELLSWORD*
GLADIATORS & THIEVES*
ASHES TO ASHES*

Short Stories
GRIMSDALR*
JACK SPRATT**
HIRAETH**

*Published by Crimson Edge
**Forthcoming by Crimson Edge

The Hawkhurst Saga

A Midwinter Sellsword

Gladiators & Thieves

Ashes to Ashes

Joshua Robertson

Chapter 1

Argus pulled the handkerchief up until it covered his nose. He could only hope that no one would recognize him. Folks had a knack for knowing a man's bloodline based on the shape of his nose. He had gone to great lengths to grow the red beard and shave his scalp, but he could not adjust his absurdly twisted, hooked nose.

He cursed his father for tormenting him with this nose.

Argus glanced sideways at Astrid Lancaster, his so-called ransom, who strutted next to him like she was leading him and not the other way around. This was not the first time Argus had kidnapped a noble lass and traded her off, but he had never known one who pottered in magic. Keeping up with the pretense that he did not believe she could turn him inside out with a twist of her wrist made him tense. The sooner he was done with her, the better.

"You won't need your handkerchief here, Mr. Gunther. They say that Hawkhurst is much warmer than the cities built on the surface." She grinned with perfectly placed, white teeth. "I never thought I would be here. There are many things to be learned. We are among the *Sevilinyth.*"

Argus fixated his gaze on the cobblestone to prevent himself from rolling his eyes. The surface-humans, the *Kedewin*, were not so different from the *Sevilinyth* living underground. The two human races were simply separated by their geography and culture. Anything said otherwise was hearsay and hogwash.

She stretched her arms over her head, bending the elbow faintly, and let out a woman's sigh. From the corner of his eye, he noticed her eyes fluttering at him when she spoke. "More importantly, we are beyond the hoarfrost and I can sleep in a warm bed tonight."

He snorted, stomping the snow from his boots cumbersomely. The woman had to recognize that he was old enough to be her father. He guessed that her flirtatious behavior was unintentional and a result of her young age.

"I might even find someone who can hold a conversation," she cooed.

He grunted. "Don't hold your breath. No one in this town is worth talking to."

"Don't be a sourpuss, Mr. Gunther. We will get the money owed to Mr. Kern and then you can return me to my father's estate. After that, you can…do whatever it is that you do. How about we visit the bank in the morning?" She hummed at the end of her question, raising the hair on the back of his neck.

"Yes." He muttered. It was the only thing he could possibly say with the hopes of putting an end to her chattering. Argus had lied to Astrid so many times in the past two months, he barely remembered telling her that acquiring a loan from the City Bank would pay her father's gambling debt.

Astrid clicked her tongue. "He really did mess up this time, didn't he? My brother warned me that his love for money would cause me trouble. Though, I never thought I would be bartered off to settle his dues. Anyway, this loan will make things right."

Argus made a sound to show he was listening. Yet, his mind was somewhere else.

"I suppose that you have been here before, then?" Astrid giggled. "I suppose Hawkhurst would be a hard place to avoid in your line of work."

Argus took a deep breath. She liked to tease him for being a sellsword, as though it made him a second-class citizen. "I have."

"I did not hear you, Darling."

He glanced up briefly to view the spiraling towers that scraped against the ceiling of the subterranean city, deep within the side of the mountain. Memories jumbled his mind at the sight, one voice screaming a name louder than the rest. It was a name he had tried to forget.

Haakan Madrin.

"Yes, Lass," he said, pushing the name out of his mind. "I have been here before."

"Then you know of a place where we could stay?"

Argus grimaced under his handkerchief. "I know a place."

A nearby guard yelled near the gate behind him and Astrid. "Move along! Move along! By the order of King Moors, move along to the interior. No drifters in Upper City. Squatters will be jailed at nightfall!"

Astrid dismissed the guard. "Is it close?"

Argus turned to see the man in plate mail shouting at the migrators who flooded through the gates behind them. The humans above ground, the *Kedewin*, were running from a civil war. Argus had been surprised when he heard that the people of Hawkhurst had given sanctum to the hundreds of refugees. It was not typical behavior for the *Sevilinyth* to show kindness, especially in response to pandemonium.

"Mr. Gunther, is the place you know close to here?"

"Nothing in Hawkhurst is close," Argus said. His words were honest. The city was built in layers, from top to bottom, from rich to poor, from free man to slave. It would take several hours to walk from one end to the other.

"Then we have plenty of time to talk. Maybe you could tell me of the *Eadfel*. My friends and I speak about it often in Galoroth."

Argus scratched his bald head. It was hard for him to believe she had any friends as much as she talked.

"I'd rather walk in silence."

"Indulge me, Mr. Gunther."

Argus swallowed, feeling as though he were at the mercy of a spoiled brat who had never had a good spanking. It was difficult to simply argue with such a person without cutting out their tongue.

Unfortunately, killing her was not part of the plan. He yielded. "The *Eadfel* is the name for the political estrangement or interrelation that occurs between the leading families in the city."

"Any simpleton could tell me that. Is it not a game?"

Argus winced. "If games end in poverty, slavery,

or death, then yes—it is a game."

Astrid crooned, a bounce in her step, "It sounds horridly delightful."

"Says a person who has never been poor, hungry, or subjugated."

"Oh?" Astrid said. Argus could not believe that the smile stayed painted on her face. She had definitely been raised in a noble house. "Do you speak from personal experience or speculation, Mr. Gunther?"

Fully armored guards with steel on their backs and belts—much like the ones that stood at the gate—passed by them on the road. He suddenly realized that more guards huddled in alleyways, flooded the streets, and dawdled about the nearby buildings. Paranoia crept down his spine. They watched for something—him.

Haakan Madrin.

His inner voice repeated the name again, causing him to shudder. He swore that he could feel the scars from old wounds begin to ache on his chest and back.

"Argus?"

Argus took another breath.

He scrunched his face, his mustache rubbing against his shagged beard. He hated the facial hair, but it was the best disguise he could muster with such short notice. "It doesn't matter."

"It does matter." Astrid tightened her pint-sized nose. "I must know if your argument comes from a place of emotion or reason."

"I am not arguing," Argus said.

Astrid opened her mouth to speak, but was drowned out by the voice in Argus's head.

Haakan Madrin.

"Shut up!" Argus bellowed at his own trailing mind before realizing he had screamed the words out loud.

The shock on Astrid's face was priceless, but Argus did not have time to relish in it. He was more concerned about the people who were suddenly staring at him.

He adjusted the handkerchief and picked up his pace.

The woman stopped smiling and matched his footfalls. Her features remained serene with the exception of her eyes. They were as cold as death. "That is not any way to speak to a person, Mr. Gunther."

Argus maintained a scowl. He almost forgot he was speaking to a mage. "Let us do each other a favor then and stop speaking all together."

Astrid didn't hesitate. "Mr. Kern will hear of this when his money is delivered."

Argus's jaw tensed at the mention of his employer's name. Astrid was like most nobles. She liked to talk—and threaten—like she knew how the day was going to unfold. The woman had no idea what Argus had arranged with Landon Kern. She would be singing something different by the end of the day. More importantly, he would be rid of her soon enough.

Argus rubbed his fingers together softly to prevent himself from pulling at his handkerchief once more. His Uncle Peter had once told him to '*keep a woman satisfied in all things except authority.*'

She did not say another word but there was a distinct, embellished exhalation that fled her lips like a strong southern wind. It was no matter. Maybe she would keep quiet long enough to get where they were going.

The two of them traveled briskly through several districts of Upper City, named after the prominent Houses. The *Scarlet Forge* caught Argus's eye within seconds of turning around the first bend in the road. He supposed that he could have taken a different path and avoided the forge altogether, but he could not come to Hawkhurst without seeing it.

The *Scarlet Forge* was owned and operated by the Sybaris family. Argus was more familiar than most with the saying that the Sybaris name was worth twice the family's fortunes. At least, it had been true until their eldest daughter had given birth to Argus thirty-five years ago. The family had left him at the gladiator pits at the age of five with his father's name and focused on squelching any rumors that might destroy their position in the city.

Argus was a bastard child—among other things. But, he had his revenge. Before he had left, he had taken care of his poor excuse for a mother.

Haakan Madrin.

He turned away from the *Scarlet Forge* in hopes that it would shield his memories. No reason to dig at old wounds.

After a few more streets, he and Astrid made it to the spiral that led downward to Middle City.

Once more, he rubbed his fingers together. Thus far, no one had approached them or had given them a second glance. He considered it a fool's luck with the knowledge that the closer they roamed to Lower City and the Cogs, the more dangerous this trek would become. He had no interest in ending the day with his head on a spike.

The sound of a woman screaming echoed against his eardrum. It was ear-piercing. Soul-crunching. Familiar.

Haakan.

"Wha—" He jerked his head briskly before realizing that the sound was another manifestation in his head. It was not real.

"Mr. Gunther?"

The man twitched uneasily before rumbling his throat at Astrid. It quickly silenced her from making any comment on his eccentric behavior. He nearly made a comment about nobles needing more training on how to keep their traps shut, but he was interrupted by the woman's scream again.

Haakan.

With a shake of his head, he pushed the noise away. He knew the woman's voice; his mother's. It took several steps before the clamor in his head desisted as though it had never been. He had to keep his wits about him! She was dead. He had made sure of it.

Argus was uncertain how much time had passed when they finally stopped in front of the dilapidated, three-story structure. He licked his lips in recognition of the old establishment. The wooden sign on metal hooks swung gently near the door at the top of a staircase. The dark lettering was newly painted against the weathered oak, *Feather Her Goose*.

He looked down the street on either side of the brothel that he faced.

Astrid mumbled incomprehensible words.

Her voice was easily drowned out by the sultry accent of the working girl who leaned against the building. "What can I do you for, Mister?" She bit her bottom lip in a half-smile, leaning against the building.

Argus barely glanced at the young girl. "I am here for Maggie."

The harlot scrunched her face in confusion.

Argus maintained his poise, nearly wanting to smack himself for the slip-up. "Madame Halum. I need to speak to the Madame."

The girl suddenly grinned like a fool. "Like your girls older, do you?" She pushed herself away from the wall, walking forward, legs crossing in front of one another. "If it is experience you are after, I am well versed."

"I'm not here for that, Lass. I just need to speak with the Madame." Argus's tone was waterless.

The girl stopped her advancement, wavering her eyes between Astrid and Argus.

She addressed Argus keenly. "Who is calling for her?"

"Argus Gunther of Hawe. She should be expecting me."

The door of *Feather Her Goose* creaked open. "I was expecting you two days ago." Madame Halum, as aged as Argus, peered from the doorway. Her soft, childish nose was nearly missed in comparison to her full lips and large green eyes. Her red hair was hidden under a purplish veil.

"There are just as many complications on the surface as in Hawkhurst."

"That I have no doubt." Madame Halum stepped back, widening the door. She was hardly friendly, speaking in a flat, shortened tone. "Come inside away from prying ears."

Argus dipped his head.

"Should I come, Madame?" The prostitute with the creamed locks curtsied from the bottom of the stairwell.

The redheaded woman glanced at Argus, leaning forward slightly with a tilt of her head as though she had just seen him. Her tone changed considerably. "This man is not for you!" The Madame raised her hand as though she would backhand the girl if she were within reach. "Inform House Oenus that the sellsword has arrived and be quick about it."

Argus shuddered nervously at the mention of the Oenus name. He wouldn't be recognized! Couldn't be! He would be in and out.

As he entered *Feather Her Goose*, he paid no attention to the prostitute scampering away from the establishment in haste. Instead, he readjusted his handkerchief for good measure.

Chapter 2

The interior design of *Feather Her Goose* had less taste than the exterior. The ceiling was cracking, the floorboards were faded, and piles of half-torn, moldy garments were scattered about the dilapidating, misplaced furniture. Strange bugs skittered from baseboard to baseboard, weaving through piles of rubble. It was hard telling but the building may have been an old house or inn before being infested with harlots.

Argus and Astrid were led through an offset door on the opposite side of a fireplace. The room that they entered was decorated with unkempt couches, the amethyst fabric tearing at the seams. There were several candles nearly burnt down to the wax casting a dim glow; it was likely meant to enhance the esthetic feel of the brothel, but for Argus, it only emitted a shadow of despair.

To his bewilderment, he guessed this was likely the finest room in the entire building.

"If it's any consolation," Astrid spoke with precision, "this is exactly what I imagined the inside would look like."

Madame Halum dipped her head. "Yes. We find that familiarity in place and practice is a prominent trademark of any business. I am glad that you approve, my Lady."

"Approve?" Astrid widened her blue eyes. "That is not what I meant."

Argus grunted in mild amusement, turning his attention towards Madame Maggie Halum, while attempting to avoid eye contact at the same time. He had known her before when they were children, a long time ago. Clearly, her affinity for the promiscuous lifestyle had not paid off. "How long until Lord Oenus arrives?"

The woman perched her chin, an indication of disbelief. She stared at Argus steadily. "You saw that I had just sent for him, Haakan. I suppose it depends on his sense of urgency in this matter."

He nearly folded, keeping his eyes off of Astrid. "It is Argus. You would do right to remember it."

The Madame's nostrils flared. She took a breath before replying, "Lose the handkerchief, Haakan. I know very well who you are, but if it is games you wish to play—so be it."

"My intent is not to play games."

The Madame spoke over him, implying that the conversation was hers to direct. After all, it was her whorehouse. "Do you think Lord Oenus will not know the bastard child of Sybaris and Madrin? There is good reason why you were thrown to the gladiator pits."

Astrid interjected, voice trembling, "What are we talking about? Are you suggesting that Mr. Gunther is not Mr. Gunther?"

Madame Halum ignored her, speaking as though

the woman was no more than horse dung beneath her stiletto. "House Oenus sits in the highest seat in Middle City and has found favor, not only with prominent Houses in Upper City, but with King Moors. The only possible threat to advancing to Upper City is House Madrin. Are you hearing me?"

Argus held himself strong, fastening his knees so his legs would not buckle. "I hear that my father and Jimi Oenus are at each other's throats. That has nothing to do with me; it never has. I am not recognized in either family."

"You carry the name. Listen, I do not know your business here, but I wonder if you have been brought here to be killed. Unless your business with Lord Oenus impacts his ascent beyond the middle class, or you have plans to betray your father, I would expect terrible things when he arrives."

Argus's throat went dry. "Then why would you send for him?"

"I put my neck out for you once, Haakan. I am too old to take those types of risks again." Her tone was like a mother telling her son why he had gotten bit after putting his hand in a dog's mouth. "You were supposed to be dead. We went through a lot of trouble to get you out."

"Do not think I am not grateful."

Argus could not expand on the thought before the woman cut him off. "No one cares about your gratitude. Take my advice and leave now. I will tell Lord Oenus that I did what I could to keep you here."

"So, you will risk it again." Argus's jaw tensed. It was all he could do to keep his own nostrils from flaring. He looked to Astrid. "I cannot leave."

The noble *Kedewin* looked frantic. For the first time since leaving Galoroth, she was actually unnerved. "You speak with the distinction of a noble, Madame Halum. What do you gain by helping…Mr. Gunther? You clearly have an investment in something."

Argus almost winced from the look the Madame gave Astrid. The expression was somewhere between bewilderment and absolute vehemence.

"Lady Lancaster," she began, "you will find the nobles in Hawkhurst do not function like the *Kedewin*. You speak like that outside of these walls and you will be flayed in the streets."

"I—"

The Madame's voice echoed. "Unlike the *Kedewin*, all *Sevilinyth* have some sense of oratory skills in this city, whether it be a noble or slave. Even a drunk on his worst day can put together a simple sentence in Hawkhurst. It is both a common and expected practice." Her next words were spoken at whisper. "So, do not mistake my simple guidance for allegiance."

Astrid puffed out her chest, which was a slight change for as small as it was. "I am not a fool, Madame! A woman does not help a man escape unless she has some sense of loyalty."

The older woman laughed. "The statement in itself is a fool's statement. I suspect you should spend a few days in Hawkhurst before playing politics."

"I am not here to play the *Eadfel*," Argus said as though the words were meant for him. "I will do what I have come to do and be gone."

"Collect a bounty?" She smiled. "If that is your

only reason here, then consider my offer forfeit. If you survive Lord Oenus, I think you will be knocking on my door again before this is all over."

Argus winced. The Madame's eyes were glued to him.

Like clockwork, a knock resounded at the door of the room. Argus nearly jumped as it swung open without invitation. From the corner of his eye, he noticed Astrid had a similar response.

"Lord Jimi Oenus, son of Samuel, of House Oenus," the harlot announced with the care of a royal herald.

The middle-aged Lord stepped into the room as though he were arriving to church mass. Clearly, he was a man of prospect, perfectly dressed with a golden-threaded, dark blue tunic. There were no loose strings. His cuffs matched his shoes. His shoes complimented his eyes. His eyes matched his social class.

Argus noticed the noble wore his allegiances openly. The symbol of House Oenus, the golden winged pennant, presented upon the Lord's left breast. The Lord's fingers each held their own jeweled bauble, including a signet ring. And, the Lord's neck displayed a massive ornament of the blood moon, the symbol of Hawkhurst, but more importantly, the symbol of the renowned Cauthe Cathedral.

Madame Halum curtsied. The shock in her eyes that the Lord had come so quickly was undetectable, but she had to be thinking it. "Lord Oenus, it is a pleasure to have you. May the sages repeat your name for as long as they have voice and their kin have memory."

Lord Oenus nodded half-heartedly to the woman.

He stayed just within the doorway, and took in the surroundings of the room, squinting with distrust.

Argus could only speculate at the power of the man. Even now, he controlled the room with his presence. His long, dirty-blonde hair touched the neck of the master-crafted lute on his back. Strangely, Argus felt all the more anxious upon seeing the musical instrument.

"Lord Oenus," Argus acknowledged, keeping his chin steady. "Argus Gunther of Hawe, under the order of Landon Kern. I have come to fulfill the charge."

Again, there was silence. The Lord scrunched his eyebrows at Astrid. Though, it was Argus who he finally settled his eyes upon.

"I have been eager to meet you, Argus Gunther, and you, Lady Lancaster."

The voice of the Lord was melodious and feminine, strikingly to the measure that Argus had to make a double-take to assure himself that it was not the Madame or harlot who had spoken.

Astrid dipped her head with clear confusion settling on her face. Her lips were sealed as though she were afraid to speak.

Argus was slower to dip his head. He could already feel himself intentionally tightening his nose, as though it would change the shape. Though, if Madame Halum had already recognized him, he may have little chance in maintaining his guise.

Lord Oenus shifted his attention. "Take your whore, Madame Halum, and leave us."

The harlot quickly fell back out of the room without further direction. Her physical discomfort mirrored what each of them were feeling.

Madame Halum curtsied again. "As you wish, my Lord."

She looked to Argus before exiting.

Once they were gone and the door was shut, Lord Oenus continued. "Explain to me why you have not come sooner. I expected you two days ago."

Argus licked his lips. "My apologies, my Lord. We should have made better time. There was misjudgment in the distance and did not account for the conflicts on the surface."

"I hope your miscalculation is not a common stance. How long have you been employed with Mr. Kern?" Lord Oenus had little reaction.

Astrid fidgeted out of the corner of his eye. Lord Oenus had not said anything about him looking like a Madrin. He might actually be able to get through the commonalities and be gone. Astrid would not have a chance to say more until he was beyond the gates.

Argus tried to be quick about his answer, quieting his rambling mind. "Eleven years and some odd change."

"From Hawe, you say?" The question nearly seemed rhetorical, challenging.

Argus focused on relaxing his face. "Aye."

"I see." The man had barely budged from the opposite end of the room. Argus tightened his arm to prevent himself from rubbing his fingers. "What is your position on the slaves within Hawkhurst? You clearly know they are the spoils of past wars…and recent?"

The Lord was obviously toying with him. Maybe he did know his real name.

Haakan Madrin.

His Uncle Peter had told him, *'truth is a precious commodity; protect it with a bodyguard of lies'.* Argus breathed steadily, palms sweating. Of course, the slaves within the lower confines of the city, the Cogs, had been citizens from Hawe before being subjugated. Argus had known as much but did not think it relevant before now. Certainly, a man like Jimi Oenus would question him on something that seemed trivial. Any type of knowledge was power in Hawkhurst.

It was a miracle the sellsword's lip did not curl, or tremble, or waver in the slightest. The Lord across from him was a statue, unblinking, watching every nonverbal cue as it slithered to the surface of Argus's body.

"I have no position on the matter, my Lord. It was not my hands that were bound, nor was I paid to fight in the war, past or present."

"Surely, your family—"

"An orphan, my Lord," he interrupted coarsely, nearly stumbling, recognizing his own insolence. Still, he continued, despite the raised eyebrow of Lord Oenus. Another saying about lying was *'never skin a rabbit halfway'.* "I have no family. Not anymore."

The emotional outburst was forgiven as the Lord spoke, seemingly touched. "My regards for your loss. Every man deserves a family. It teaches him obligation beyond what the state can demand; it is a visceral feeling, seeing your blood flow in the veins of your own. Brother or child, the connection found in a relationship holds absolute sway over a man."

"Yes, my Lord. I could not imagine." The words were more difficult for Argus to utter than his last. He breathed deeply, hoping it was perceived as emotional dishevel and not anything more. He felt his mustache scrape against his beard, and consciously relaxed the muscles in his face.

Lord Oenus dropped his chin. "There is also family beyond blood. Maybe someday you will know it."

Argus returned the gesture with some simple phrase of gratitude. He hardly knew what he had said, but the Lord across from him dipped his head once more. Argus flinched. When a noble shows a simple man kindness, it generally comes with a blade in the back. '*It is not the nature of an asp to bite without its poison.*'

Astrid, clearly dissatisfied with the conversation, piped up, "What does this have to do with anything? Why are you here?"

Argus swallowed. He knew he could count on the young lass to press things along.

"To business, then," Lord Oenus said. His hand comfortably rested on his waist as he spoke. "The agreement is as follows. The two of you are to serve my house. I will cover necessary expenses. I will also expedite punishment where it is deserved. You will not approach the Oenus estate or my family unless receiving word with my insignia. I have made arrangements for you to stay at *Creon's Inn.*"

Argus clenched his jaw before quickly interjecting, "My apologies, but I believe you have misunderstood the arrangement. My task is to deliver Lady Lancaster to you. I am not part of the contract."

"The arrangement was for two, not one. I am afraid it is you who is misunderstood."

"Excuse me?" Astrid cried. "We have plans to go to the bank!"

Argus's chest swelled noticeably, ignoring her and raising his voice. Landon Kern had him enslaved. "I am a free man."

"No more." Lord Oenus's voice was eerily composed, like a minstrel telling the worse part of a story – with even keel – to add emphasis to the tragic unfolding within the plot.

"I will fetch you another body, if that is what you desire. There are plenty within Hawkhurst, I am sure of it." Argus fumed, his fingers pressed together firmly.

"I'm afraid there is no bartering here. You were a part of the original agreement."

Astrid screeched, "I am not a slave! I am a noble from Galoroth and will be treated as such!"

Lord Oenus abruptly sneered, moving like lightening, his fingers gripping the neck of his instrument on his back ominously. "Remove your hands from your weapon!"

Argus gasped, turning to face Astrid, but the woman did not carry a weapon. Of course, a mage would not hold a blade.

He quickly realized he was holding the metallic hilt of the long sword at his belt. He lifted his hand away. Were his fingers not just pressed together?

If he killed the Lord of a noble House, it would take more than dumb luck to make it out of Hawkhurst alive.

Lord Oenus did not free his own grip, fingers wrapped around the musical instrument like it was the sword of swords. His voice was level, again, but any sense of compassion he may have presented before was lost. "You and your companion will be compensated half-wages for your *support*, Mr. Gunther. Do not think of me as callous. Though, the two of you will repay Mr. Kern's debt to me through labor. There is too much to risk otherwise."

Astrid licked her lips, suddenly having more sense about her than either man. "What is the debt amount? I can still obtain a loan from the bank in the morning and take care of this matter once and for all."

"The price is not measured in coin but in my personal gain...a thing Mr. Kern has obstructed in the past."

"So we are serving you to pay a debt from Kern, whilst we serve Mr. Kern to pay a debt to my father?" Astrid asked.

Lord Oenus let go of his lute. "Quite a web, is it not?"

Astrid did the only thing any person could do in this moment, which infuriated Argus all the more. She smiled. "What is it you need done?"

Lord Oenus reached inside his pocket for a crumpled piece of parchment and handed it to Argus.

Argus unfolded the letter.

Lord Jimi Oenus,

> You will terminate your involvement in Upper City, lest you wish to continue to collect your daughter in chunks. You have a fortnight to consider before receiving another piece. What is left of Lillian Oenus will be released upon your resignation of title, fortune, and lands.

Lord Aaron Quist

Argus could not help but sneer at the Lord through

gritted teeth. "That is quite the unfortunate circumstance."

Lord Oenus continued, "Lilly went missing nearly a week ago. We received this in a package delivered from the *Bracken and Pine* two days ago."

He tossed an object at Argus, who quickly caught it in the air. It only took a moment before he noticed it was a severed finger. He did not flinch.

Astrid convulsed upon seeing the bloodied limb as though she may vomit.

"I do not think it is my daughter's, but I must be certain. You are to find Lilly and those responsible for her disappearance."

Astrid stumbled to Argus's side and took the letter from him.

"Do you believe Lord Quist is responsible?" Argus asked.

"We don't know what to think exactly, as there has been no visible irregular activity from House Quist."

"This is ridiculous! Why don't you just contact the guard to investigate?" Astrid asked, gaining her senses once more. "Seems they would be able to investigate better than a couple random *Kedewin*."

Lord Oenus grimaced. "Involving the authorities would prove detrimental to the long-term objectives of House Oenus. They should not be involved in the investigation."

Astrid smirked. "You mean to say it will stall the advancement of your House into Upper City? You do not want to be seen as too weak to manage your own affairs?"

"There are evidently loose tongues amuck in Hawkhurst." Lord Oenus's face reddened. "I need skilled hands that are not involved in the politics in this city to pursue this matter. Anyone else may be corrupted."

"I suspect that refusal to do so, attempts to escape, and the like will end with death or worse?" The sardonic tone in Argus's speech was unmistakable. However, he considered his attitude to be obligatory with the given situation.

"Yes, your station is unfortunate, but hear me when I promise you it could be much worse." The man's voice was imposing and menacing in the same breath.

It was in that moment Argus decided he was going to kill Jimi Oenus.

Chapter 3

Argus knew the road to murdering Jimi Oenus was long and treacherous, but it might also be the only way to leave Hawkhurst. He did not want to be trapped within the city. If this was anything like the last time, he would have a handful of individuals he would have to cut through to get out. The thought added to his sour mood.

He gulped the last drop from the oversized tankard of stout before waving at the wench to bring him another. *Creon's Inn* was disgustingly dark and thick, but he wanted to be drunk. Argus chomped into another biscuit to dull the taste while glaring across the table at Astrid, who attempted to swallow down her own meal.

"You were really going to consign me to the service of another man without my father's consent? Is Mr. Kern really that foolish?" Astrid sipped lightly from her honeyed wine with a raised eyebrow. Her dark curls bounced slightly as she licked the leftover liquid from the edge of her lips. "My father trusted you."

Argus stared off at nothing, disregarding the lass

and her complaining. The night had been long and burdensome, with little comfort and even less sleep. Astrid had spent the evening hours in silence, fuming in the way that women did. Now that morning had come, she had found use for her tongue once more.

"He was a fool to think you would be true to your word. My mother, bless her soul, would have never allowed this to happen. You just wait until my brother hears of this—what Mr. Kern has done—what you have done. He will burn this city to ashes to find me," she muttered between bites.

Argus ignored her, scanning the vicinity. The building was wide with plenty of space for the patrons to flounder about, making a complete nuisance of themselves. They were almost loud enough to block out Astrid's girly whining. The only thing more annoying than her voice was the deafening clanging from outside the building.

Creon's Inn was situated in the heart of Middle City, within the gaze of House Oenus, between *Lady Sophia Arms* and *Rusty Blade*. Argus remembered the businesses well. He had received provisions from each of them when he had been fighting in the arena with the other gladiators. They were memories he preferred not to think about. Still, he never could figure out what would compel a person to build a place of rest and relaxation between a blacksmith and weapons shop.

"I am talking to you, Mr. Gunther!" Astrid squawked louder than necessary, her hand slapping against the tabletop angrily. "Or, should I refer to you by your real name?"

"Astrid!" Argus cautioned, scratching his head off-handedly.

The room quieted as the customers turned from their tables. But when nothing more came from the disruption, the men and women returned to their food, drinks, and idle chatter.

Argus adjusted his food to cover his face, and waited until it appeared the majority had lost interest in them. He finally mumbled, "Yes, I planned on handing you off to Lord Oenus. I did not know the full details of it. I am a sellsword, Lass. I follow instructions and receive payment. That's it!"

"You were a sellsword," she corrected. "Now, you are a slave like me."

Argus glowered. "No need to be hateful." He did not want to tell her that he knew what it meant to be a slave. He tried to reason with her instead. "We are in this together, and it will take us working together to escape this cursed city."

Astrid widened her eyes, intrigued by the simple concept. She slid her chair back, preparing to stand upright. "Then, let us leave this city and be done with this!"

"No." Argus said, scrunching his beard to his mustache. "It is not that easy."

"Why not?" Astrid rustled, her eyes full of fire, lips pursed.

The wench approached the table casually, sitting down the tankard for Argus. He dropped a couple coins for her and waved her away from the table.

"Why not?" Astrid repeated in her crisp manner, not seeming to understand the need for caution.

Argus motioned for her to lean forward to hear his whisper. Reluctantly, she scooted her chair back to the table. Argus kept his tone at a whisper. "There are eyes everywhere in this city. Do not be surprised if every word you speak is heard and reported back to Lord Oenus within an hour."

Astrid parted her lips in disbelief. "Alright, Argus. While we are speaking in the realm of folk tales, why don't you tell me how you know these things? What exactly is your connection in Hawkhurst? Madame Halum said you were the son of Sybaris and Madrin, which must mean something. Tell me, who are you really?"

Argus pulled back tenuously. He looked around the room like a trapped animal. "I will help you escape with me, if you do not ask me these questions. You do not know what you are risking by talking about such things out here."

"You expect me to trust you after what has transpired? I have the right to know."

"You don't have much of a choice."

She batted her eyes, and gawked. "Neither do you." Her dark curls fell out of place on either side of her cold eyes. Her gaze was locked on Argus.

"I am a bastard son, an orphan, and was a gladiator in the Arena. I have a fancy name with no weight." Argus snorted.

"Argus Gunther," a man, larger than life, said as he plumped himself down in a chair at the table. Even sitting, he was massive in height and breadth. The man dried a mug with a hand towel offhandedly, smiling wildly, looking him and Astrid carefully with beady eyes.

The sellsword lifted his eyes warily, aware of what words he had just shared with Astrid. "What can I do you for?"

"I am Creon Nass, owner of this here place. I understand House Oenus has made the arrangements to pay for your stay. Any fool knows they don't hand out their coin for free. No trouble, I hope?"

Argus instinctively put his hand on the hilt of his sword, taking in the full measure of the so-called innkeeper. The man was wide but not fat. He was built like a warrior, his right arm covered in banded armor. As odd as it was, it was the half-crescent moon axe hanging from his fine leather belt that really drew Argus's attention.

Astrid was the most surprised. "You are the innkeeper?"

"Aye. I imagine I don't look much like it." It was true. The man had as many healed wounds on him as Argus, if not more, and was about twice the size in muscle. "I spend my free time in the Arena." He winked before spitting into the mug and scrubbing.

Astrid pointedly pushed her own mug away. "A gladiator, then?"

"I am. A free gladiator unlike those poor slaves from Hawe. I choose to fight in the Arena."

"What a ridiculous thing to do!" Astrid widened her eyes.

Creon raised an eyebrow. "It is a more honorable way to achieve a living than most, especially here in Hawkhurst."

"I suppose there is some truth to that," she said.

The innkeeper tapped the mug on the table momentarily before addressing Argus. "You look awfully familiar to me. Are you from around here?"

Argus gulped, quickly changing the subject. "We expect to stay clear of trouble, Creon. Are you generally so concerned about your patrons and their affiliations?"

Creon grunted. "Of course I am. Businesses can come and go in this city without warning. I've seen many burn to the ground or worse from disputing guilds and houses alike. I'd rather my inn not meet the same fate."

"Fair enough," Astrid said quietly. "Maybe you can point us in the right direction."

"There is no need," Argus said briskly, shushing the noble woman. It was all he needed for her to start spreading the business of House Oenus all over the city. "We appreciate your hospitality, Creon. Good day."

It was about as kind of a dismissal as Argus could muster.

Creon noticeably winced at being shooed away from the two, especially in his inn, but he stood up from the table anyhow. Though, he leaned back down and spoke gruffly, "I come with counsel. Neither of you are to attempt to flee this city through force, magic, or otherwise. You are being watched and such an act will not be tolerated by House Oenus."

Astrid's jaw dropped. "Who told you to say this to us? Lord Oenus?"

Argus tried to shush the woman with his gaze. She seemed to take the hint.

Creon grunted, replacing his solemn look with a wide grin once more. "If there is anything you need while you are under my roof, do not hesitate to ask."

The man dipped his head with a grimace painted on his face, and then retreated to check on other customers.

Astrid frowned. "What was that about? Are we really being threatened by Lord Oenus?"

"Why not? It makes sense for him to keep us down while he can."

"I had thought about using magic to get us out of the city. Maybe teleport us beyond the walls if we could find a few more magi to maintain the spell, but I was not sure if you could be trusted. Honestly, I am still not convinced."

"You do not heed warnings well, do you?" Argus scowled. "That plan would not work here anyway. The magi in the Ascension are the only ones who use magic here and they have wards to stop its misuse."

"I notice that you ignored my statement about trusting you."

Argus gripped his tankard. "Don't trust anyone. You will live longer."

Astrid shifted in her chair, raising her eyebrow. "I see. It seems finding Lillian Oenus is our only means of escape. Though, this city is too massive to randomly start looking for a single person."

"Lord Oenus gave us plenty of information to begin our search. Just remember, this will be smoother if we can keep ourselves away from public attention."

"Very well, Mr. Gunther. We will do it your way. Where do we start?"

Argus thought the answer was clear, but he said the words anyway. "The *Bracken and Pine*."

Chapter 4

The warehouse known as the *Bracken and Pine* was located in Middle City, a simple stretch away from *Creon's Inn*. The three-storied building loomed over the path of the street, taking over a block and a half. It was simple in design but powerful in its overall mass.

"I don't understand the purpose of this oversized warehouse. Don't the individual businesses and guilds in the city keep their own goods?" Astrid asked. "Why would people accumulate their goods and bring them here? That is not the way business is done."

"It is the way in Hawkhurst." Argus said flatly as they walked. He peered in several directions, keeping his handkerchief drawn up tight. "Guilds don't have the same role here as they might on the surface. The system here isn't built to co-operate but to compete. If we are going to get out of here, you need to forget what it is like in Galoroth. You need to forget the ways of the *Kedewin*."

"What do you mean?"

"I mean a lot of things." Argus muttered. "For instance, the *Bracken and Pine* is a Merchant Guild, built on capitalistic values. They hold goods, sell goods, deliver goods, and so forth. They are also an inner-city marketplace for trade, but not just goods. They will also sell information. This warehouse has changed the balance of social classes over the past half century in Hawkhurst. It has given room for the proprietors and commoners, separating them from the paupers and slaves of the lower districts. Don't be mistaken, though. It is the nobles who still hold power in Hawkhurst."

"You nearly sound like a noble yourself." The woman's voice was clearly intrigued. "Where has this been during the past few months? You have barely talked. Besides, I thought you said you were an orphan and a gladiator."

Argus grunted.

"That's the sound I am used to," Astrid dipped her voice, "but it is not an answer. I can only imagine how the *Bracken and Pine* factors in with the *Eadfel*."

Argus smacked his lips, noticing she was referencing the political 'game' again. He rightly did not care about her fascination with it, as long as it kept the subject on something other than him. "Yes, it is another element of the *Eadfel*. And, we are stuck right in the middle of it."

She responded, reflecting further, "What gain was there by adjusting the social structure here? Really, I don't understand why the leaders of Hawkhurst would disguise the status of royalty and the role of the people within the kingdom. The regular system has worked successfully for centuries on the surface. Besides, what has really changed?"

"Everything was gained. It changed the people's perception of the source of their suffering. The

Kedewin blame their fate on the kings. The *Sevilinyth* believe their suffering is the result of their own poor choices. It makes it less likely for a revolt against those who rule."

"But, it is a falsehood?"

Argus agreed. "Of course it is. But, it keeps the sheep from bleating too loud. The nobles in power gain their riches and live in luxury. The rest think they are free while having no freedom at all."

"So, it is all a ruse. The whole concept of freedom, choice, and self-determination is written to maintain power and control." Astrid slowed her pace. "But, surely it works sometimes. I mean, someone has to advance beyond their station every so often."

"Sure, once in a while, you have a beggar become a store owner or a slave who finds liberation." Argus paused, biting his inner cheek. He nearly let the words of his past slip from his tongue. "You have to in order to give people hope in the system. But, the changes are never so grand to actually make a difference. It is much like the debates you may hear among the nobles regarding social rights. Social rights can change repeatedly over time, but nothing really changes when wealth and power are maintained in the same way. Social rights are a distraction to the masses so they will be diverted from the real issues. This way, they will not recognize their own slavery—thinking they are free as long as they are not wearing chains."

The noble woman stopped.

Haakan Madrin.

The words screamed in his head. He shivered with a twitch. He wanted to know why he could not stop thinking those two words.

Astrid kept going, "Why don't the aristocrats rule with goodness and help the people beneath them?"

Argus nearly laughed at the notion. "Aren't you a noble? You should know decent people are the pawns of the self-serving. Good people are betrayed, forsaken, and die alone."

"That is not true."

Argus responded in a guttural tone. "Sure it is, Lass. Else, you would not be in this mess."

The sellsword could hear the woman exhale behind him. "Then, perhaps, we do have something in common after all."

"You say a lot of stupid things," Argus said, flaring his nostrils. "But don't call me a good man."

Several young men, half the age of Argus, stood near the large double doors marking the entrance to the *Bracken and Pine*. One lad with dark hair and darker eyes separated from the group and approached him and Astrid.

"Morning, Stranger. What can I do you for?"

"I need to speak with the owner," Argus said.

"You want to speak to Link Sangrey. My apologies, Stranger. He will be out of town for the better half of a month. Went on an adventure to the Underverse."

Argus pursed his lips at the mention of the world beneath Hawkhurst. Very few traversed to the depths of the world beneath and lived to tell about it. "Who is in charge while he is away?"

"What do you want to know for?" The young man smiled. "You aren't from around here?"

Astrid placed a hand on her hip. "What makes you say that?"

The man peered over his shoulder momentarily before answering. "For one, you don't know who I am."

Argus and Astrid said nothing, waiting for the inevitable.

As expected, he continued, "Thorin Awklee. I am the personal courier to House Etha. I know everyone in this town and they know me."

"Good for you," Argus said flatly. He did his best to play dumb. House Etha was one of the more powerful houses in Middle City, but more importantly, it was aligned with his father's house, House Madrin. Of course, this meant House Etha was in opposition to House Oenus. Argus was not going to get any information from Thorin.

Haakan Madrin.

Argus rubbed his fingers together to prevent himself from screaming. The voice was getting louder. It pounded like a sword against a shield.

Thorin frowned.

Astrid echoed Argus, "Who is in charge, Darling?"

The courier spit, his feelings seemingly shattered from being disrespected. "Tolliver Wolfram. You can find him inside but I doubt he will want to talk to you."

Argus moved to walk around the boy but was caught by Thorin's hand on his shoulder. "If you cannot get the information you need from Tolliver, come and speak with me."

"Thanks, Kid." Argus said, taking several more steps to push past the young man. The last thing he wanted to do was spend time around someone affiliated with the Etha family. Enough coin might buy Thorin off, but it would also be the quickest way to be recognized from House Madrin.

The interior of the warehouse looked as one would expect with rows of goods and columns of crates. There were very few men who moved around within the building.

Argus called out to one of them. "Tolliver?"

The man shook his head, and pointed further back into the warehouse. Argus looked beyond the worker, spotting an office with paned windows in the back.

He weaved in and out of the rows with Astrid gliding behind him. "Lot of crannies for prying ears within these walls," Argus said beneath his breath.

Astrid hummed in agreement.

It was not until Argus stepped into the mediocre office that the man called Tolliver raised his green eyes from a stack of papers. He glanced between Argus and Astrid, and then to a yellow-skinned man on his left.

Tolliver clicked his tongue on the roof of his mouth, and dropped his eyes back to the papers. His thin graying hair hung down to his light-colored eyebrows. "Good day. How can I help you?"

Argus bit his inner cheek before answering with a question. "Are you Tolliver Wolfram?"

"I am."

"I need information regarding a package you delivered to House Oenus."

Tolliver didn't even hesitate in shuffling his papers. If he was pretending to be engrossed in his work, he was doing a nice job of it. "The *Bracken and Pine* delivers lots of packages, Mister. We take payment and deliver as directed. Some are recorded transactions and some are not, depending on who is doing the transaction. We seldom know the contents of any letter or package unless we transcribe it ourselves. I am not sure what you are after, but I assure you it is unlikely you will find it here."

Astrid slapped her hand on her hip. "What is with the attitude? We haven't even asked a question yet."

"Abdul can show you back the way you came," Tolliver said.

The tall man in the corner shifted his weight expectantly. He stood well above Argus, but had less muscle. The sellsword had fought bigger.

Argus rubbed his beard to keep his hand off of his sword hilt. He did not like Tolliver's tone any more than Astrid did.

He pressed, "The letter said it was delivered by House Quist. Have you delivered any packages for the Quist family recently?"

Tolliver stood up, his shoulders scrunched up and sunk again before he gathered his papers into his hands. The man was probably ten years older than Argus, but had an air of deftness about him. He spoke with heated breath. "Like I said, we don't keep records of all our transactions. We definitely do not track the dealings with the noble houses. Now, if you will excuse me."

Argus fumed. "No, I will not. Who does the dealings with the noble houses? Their memory will serve as record well enough, and if it does not, I will cut it from their skull."

That got Tolliver's attention. The gray-haired man considered Argus with a shrewd glance. The warehouse manager was not scared. No, he was attentive, his eyes gleaming. "Threats, is it? Why don't you tell me your name, Mister?"

Argus found himself trying to change the shape of his nose once more. "I am asking the questions here, Tolliver. Tell me, who had the package sent to the Oenus family?"

He smirked and nodded to his lackey, who stepped in front of Argus. The corner of Tolliver's mouth arched as he talked. "If the letter said House Quist, Mister, then I would guess that would be your answer. Why don't you pester them with your inquiries, Mister Madrin?"

Argus's jaw tightened. He froze.

Haakan Madrin! His mother's dying voice echoed again in his ears.

"What did you call me?" Argus jumbled, swiping his finger across his nose. This time he did not stop himself from letting his hand continue downward for his sword.

Abdul's hand hastily caught his wrist to stop him from drawing the weapon. Argus swatted his hand away with a growl.

"Stop," Astrid warned from the rear. It was not clear who she was talking to.

Tolliver lifted his voice. "Did you not think I would know you, Haakan. I watched you fight from the stands of the Arena fifteen years ago. A noble and a slave. There are not many from Hawkhurst who can carry those titles simultaneously."

"I don't know you," Argus said. He had no interest in arguing with the man about his nobility.

If everyone else recognizes you, why doesn't Lord Oenus? Maybe, he does and has said nothing.

The thought sent a chill up his neck.

"Of course you don't. You have no reason to know

me, but it is my duty to know people. I was born in the Cogs. My sister is a slave and a gladiator who fights within the dome. Yes, you are known well to me, Mister. You are an arrogant and deceitful, double-crossing man! There is nothing I can do for you here."

Argus cried out against the insult. His mind was clouded as he pushed Abdul in the chest, causing the man to stumble backwards a couple of feet. The sellsword took the chance to jerk free his blade. He could not let either of these men live. They knew his face, his identity. They would tell his secret.

Haakan Madrin.

Images of his bloodied hands over her pale skin filled his vision. The sound of her screams echoed in his eardrums.

Argus kicked the desk, barely hearing Astrid's outcry from behind him. The desk slid into Tolliver, knocking the man into the wall.

Tolliver grunted in surprise as he was pinned, but Argus could not advance forward. Abdul was quicker to react than anticipated, nearly with inhuman speed, flashing in front of Argus once more. The large man's fist collided into Argus's gut followed by a second strike to the temple.

Argus accepted the strikes. Images of past battles in the Arena melded with the present. He pictured Erik Blinck crossing the sands of the circular battlefield with his serrated daggers. The crowd roared and clapped in anticipation. The man had been quick with his punches; the deadly blades had left deep scars on his back. Argus had bled for days.

Haakan Madrin.

Abdul struck Argus in the side of the head again

when the sellsword did not fall. Argus was overwhelmed by other memories. He envisioned Kor Lorik, the Iron Mask, with his crescent-shaped cleavers. The knife-edges had left their imprints on his calves and midsection. Argus relived the stunning blows that the bear of a man had delivered to his ribcage, his face. His nose had been broken along with four ribs on his left side. The battle had been long and bloody, but Argus had been victorious. Argus always won.

Another blow to his body only infuriated Argus. Returning to reality, he threw a knee up into Abdul's groin. As the man doubled over, Argus spun his sword like a quarterstaff, connecting the hilt with Abdul's jaw. He fully expected the man to fall unconscious. Instead, the lackey's eyes flashed white as though they were energized by pure energy.

There was more to Abdul then Argus had guessed. The man was a mage. He pulled his arm back with intent to thrust the sword into the midsection of his enemy.

"Stop!" Astrid demanded, pulling on Argus's bicep and pushing Abdul from harm's way with her other hand. Her face was reddened and twisted. Argus could not guess how long she had been trying to break them apart.

With a quick reflection across the room, he decided it could not have been long. Tolliver was still trying to free himself from behind the desk.

"We can help each other." Astrid breathed with the grace of a noble woman. "Be reasonable!"

His Uncle Peter's voice echoed *only the grace of a woman can cool a man's boiling blood.*

Tolliver words were heavy, exhaled between his pursed lips. "How so?"

"We will free your sister."

Argus jerked his head around. "We cannot do that!"

"Impossible." Tolliver said.

"No, it can be done." Astrid assured. "I swear to you; it will be done. Tell me her name."

Tolliver's jaw dropped, looking to Abdul, who said nothing. The tall man's eyes were locked on Argus's lifted sword, warily.

"Lower your weapon, Haakan," Tolliver whispered, his eyes darting to look out the pane glass and back again.

Argus followed his gaze, seeing nothing. "Stop calling me that."

Tolliver shied back in confusion. "What should I call you then?"

"Argus…" he said, sheathing his sword. "Argus Gunther."

"Very well," Tolliver said, facing Astrid. "And what of you with the empty promises?"

"My name is Astrid Lancaster from Galoroth, and I keep to my word."

"You travel in the company of a man who does not." Tolliver pushed at the desk again without any luck. Abdul stepped sideways and repositioned the obstruction with ease, giving Tolliver the freedom to move about. "I do not have any reason to believe you."

"I—"

Tolliver did not let Astrid interject. "However, I will say this. If you free my sister, I will help you. I will find out who sent the package to House Oenus."

Astrid nodded. "Who is she?"

"Her name is Karine. In the Arena, they call her Karine the Swift."

"Done!" Astrid said.

"Not done," Argus said with equal force.

Astrid glared at him. "It is done, Tolliver. We will return soon with your sister. In the meantime, I trust you will keep…Argus's identity to yourself, yes?"

Tolliver dipped his head. "As I do with all things, my Lady."

Satisfied, Astrid made her way out of the office and back towards the entrance of the warehouse. She did not say a word but simply left.

Argus frowned, not knowing what to say. He cocked his head at Tolliver, who stared back with a half-smile. There were no words. No statement, diplomatic or threatening, would change what had just transpired.

After a moment, he grumbled, "Be sure you keep my name concealed, Tolliver. It would be a shame for the Ascension to find out you are hiding a sorcerer within the *Bracken and Pine*."

The smirk on the manager's face turned sour as he took a glimpse toward Abdul.

Argus growled, gesturing his departure, and followed the woman.

Chapter 5

"Are you out of your mind?" Argus fizzed between his teeth as they began their way back down the road towards *Creon's Inn.* "There is no way to free his sister, Astrid. You are going to get us killed."

"Don't talk to me, Argus," she said. "I do not even know who you are."

"You don't need to know who I am!"

Some folks in the street looked in their direction. Argus hung his head as if he could hide from their gaze.

Astrid spun around in the street. He had to take a step back to avoid her hitting him. "Yes, I do. You have a history here and I need to know what we are up against. People recognize you at every turn."

Argus squinted, peering into the woman's eyes. He kept his voice as low as he possibly could, holding back his anger. "We would not be up against anything, if you would keep your mouth closed. This is not the place or time to be having this conversation, Astrid!"

She lifted her chin, raising her finger and striking him in the chest. "You started this, Argus! I came to Hawkhurst to go to the bank. Not to go on a wild goose chase!"

"Keep walking," he said. People had stopped in the street to literally watch them.

She exasperated and made a noise Argus could not describe. It was between the sound of a roaring wind and a dying cat.

He turned white in response while Astrid spun on her heel, strutting off down the cobblestone. The woman was untamable.

She did not make it more than half a block when several arrows zinged by her head. One nearly struck her cheek. She stumbled back in amazement.

The citizens around them screamed.

"Get down!" Argus shouted. He followed the trajectory of the arrows. Two had come from the rooftop and one from the alleyway. He spotted two figures duck down from the roof just as another arrow was launched from the alley.

With two steps, he flew through the air and tackled Astrid, slamming her against the dirt. The arrow whizzed by his ear as they clamored into a heap.

She wheezed, the wind knocked from her lungs.

Argus was back to his feet and moving before the noble woman could regain her breath enough to curse. His sword found its way into his right hand as he sprinted to the small road between the buildings. He whipped around the corner into the shadows.

In seconds, he was face to face with a hooded figure trying frantically to nock another arrow. The man apparently had seen him coming, but was not fast enough to respond.

The sellsword swiped the sword downwards, cutting through the longbow when the man attempted to block the attack.

"Please, I—"

Argus didn't flinch in jabbing the sword into the man's chest. The bastard only yelled for a moment before falling back off the blade. Blood oozed onto the city street.

Argus ignored the mess and turned back to face the street. The simple movement was just enough to dodge another arrow that zinged by him. Luck was on his side. Another arrow scraped by his elbow and missed.

He hated archers. They were about the closest thing to cowards that a man could face on the battlefield.

He zigzagged out into the open of the main road, keeping his eyes on the two hooded figures firing at him from the rooftops. He had been well-trained to fight against ranged weapons. He dove and spun clear from the arrows as he had in his years in the Arena. It only took one time of taking a few arrows to the leg before he learned to be lighter on his feet.

"Come on," he sneered. He searched for a path to the rooftop. None was immediately evident. The yellow bellies would have to come down eventually unless they were up there crafting arrows.

He heard shouts from the surrounding *Sevilinyth* to bring the guard. That was all he needed, the military to flood the streets and drag him off. He knew it would not take long for the armored guards to make their way to Middle City, if they weren't here already. He and Astrid had to get off the streets.

"Astrid!"

The noble woman was back on her feet and facing the hooded assailants on the rooftops. Argus suddenly noticed a blue glow illuminating her two hands while she mumbled under her breath.

Argus could not believe it. She was actually going to use her craft within Hawkhurst.

"Astrid, stop!"

She did not hear him, or if she did, she did not care to listen. In an instant, indigo-colored fireballs spiraled from her hands towards the archers. Argus could only watch in absolute horror.

Neither man had a chance against the magical energy that struck them. Argus was not even certain they had seen it coming. Blue flames ignited upon impact, searing through fabric, skin, and bone. Their screams flooded the streets. One of them leaped from the roof and collided head first into the cobblestone. The flames still singed. The second continued wailing for several seconds until he fell backwards from Argus's sight, followed by silence.

Argus fled to Astrid, grabbing her roughly by her loose clothing. "Get out of here, Astrid. You don't know what you have done."

The noble woman jerked away from him. "I protected myself, Argus. The same as you."

"No," he started. "You…you used magic."

"So what?" she said coldly.

"It's forbidden here!"

Astrid flung her mask upwards. "What are you talking about? Magic exists everywhere. Hawkhurst is home of the Ascension. There is magic here, too."

Argus did not have a chance to respond before flashes of light began to surge within the street. Energy swelled between him and Astrid, throwing him away from her. He propelled and rotated through the air, sword flying from his grip, and crashed into the side of a building.

He creaked, trying to lift himself to his feet. It was impossible. The magic engulfing the area held him at bay. He was lucky he could hold his eyes open to watch the scene unfold.

A bulb of purplish fire ballooned around Astrid, protecting her from the white stripes of light bouncing about the street like lightning. Several strands struck the magical shield, but it did not waver against the conflicting energy.

Astrid held her body rigid, perturbed by what was happening, but her facial features were serene. She was as composed as could be expected within her fortress of magic.

As if testing her resiliency, the fabric of space ripped apart in several places around Astrid. As if connecting one place with another, a handful of men and women in black wraps, and crimson mantles, emerged from the magical splice that formed. The symbol of the Cauthe Cathedral, the blood moon, gleamed from the hanging ornament across each of their chests.

"Run," Argus tried to shout again, but his voice was squandered by the vibrating energy. He realized he was not the only one who was restrained by the magic-users. Anyone who was within the vicinity was being restrained to prevent any unwarranted interference. The sorcerers from the Ascension were powerful, having a direct link with Cauthe, the Prince of Darkness.

Ten magi surrounded Astrid. With the cackling white light, Argus could not tell if words were exchanged or not. He pushed with all his might to stand but it was futile. He could not budge.

A dark mist emitted from nothingness, veiling those from the Ascension and Astrid. It was as dark as a storm cloud. Then, as quickly as it had formed, there was a thunderclap and it dispersed along with the magi and Astrid.

Argus's invisible restraints were gone. He stood slowly, bewildered. He could barely believe what had just happened. Astrid was gone.

"Should have expected as much when they opened the gates to the *Kedewin*. Surfacers don't know the law," said one *Sevilinyth*.

"I hope she burns," another said.

Argus turned away as more citizens returned to their feet, muttering under their breath, and returning to their daily grind. He stumbled over to his sword and jammed it back into the scabbard on his belt.

He was stunned.

He had no way to save Astrid. To maintain his secret identity, he had a promise to Tolliver he had to keep. Not to mention, he was in the service of the most powerful house in Middle City and had come no closer to solving the disappearance of Lillian Oenus. This was turning out to be a rotten day.

"Are you the man in service of House Oenus?" a cracked voice said over his shoulder.

Argus swallowed hard. Nothing pleasant would come from a conversation starting with those words.

"Who is asking?" He spoke under his breath, refusing to turn his head around.

"Syomin Ekdal."

Argus frowned, keeping his eyes forward. The man was from the only house of influence in Lower City.

House Ekdal managed the thieves' guild, several brothels, and the gladiator arena. A lifetime ago, they had been Argus's employer.

"What does the *Hand of Tear'n* want with my business?"

"That depends. Are you are interested in knowing why the hunters have attacked you in the open?"

Argus kept his back to Syomin. "How much would that information cost me?"

A female's voice resounded behind him. "Consider it free. They don't want you to find me."

Argus spun around. "Nothing in Hawkhurst is free." His eyes met with a young girl who could be no other than Lillian Oenus.

Her brown eyes were round and soft beneath her green hood. But, it was her companion, Syomin Ekdal, who looked the most surprised. His long black locks, several braided, barely swayed. His vocal cords had a difficult time forming the single word.

"Haakan."

Chapter 6

Argus Gunther settled against the wooden frame of his seat within the thieves' guildhouse. The hair on his forearms stood on end. His memory was a bit fuzzy as to how he had come to this place. The short skirmish with the *Hunter's Guild* and the mages abducting Astrid Lancaster was fresh in Argus's mind. He even remembered following Syomin Ekdal out of Middle City. Yet, he could not remember actually coming to the guildhouse. It was a strange sensation to know where he was without remembering how he had come to be there.

The chair groaned under his frame. He held his feet firmly to the ground to balance his weight, while trying to give the impression he was completely relaxed. In truth, he was as calm as a sheep about to be castrated.

"How long have you been in the city, Haakan?" Syomin Ekdal said, clicking his tongue on the roof of his mouth. The master thief had gained a bit of his composure since exiting Middle City. At first, the man had appeared startled at the sight of Argus. He could not blame him. It had been fifteen years since they had seen one another. Yet, Syomin now had a complete sense of calm as though it were customary for Argus to be visiting him in his quarters.

Argus shrugged his shoulders, taking in the piles of broken trinkets littering the desk before him. Similar items of little value were scattered across the floorboards. It astonished him that the thieves stole junk far more than jewels.

"Haakan?" Syomin repeated Argus's real name. It was a name Argus had deserted years ago when he had left the subterranean city.

When he provided no response, Syomin added at an even pace, "It speaks wonders that the *Hand of Tear'n* wasn't your first stop, especially considering what House Ekdal had done to aid your escape." Syomin unstrapped his leather shoulder pads and handed them to the third party in the room, Lillian Oenus.

Argus eyed her delicate movements unsure of when she may have entered through the side door. When thinking of it, he did not remember coming in through the door himself.

Lillian was his target. He had spent the past day searching for the noble lass at the direction of her father, Lord Oenus. She was supposed to be in great peril. Clearly, it was not the case.

He was bewildered.

Lillian looked at him wide eyed as she gathered the armor from Syomin. At closer inspection, Argus decided there was sadness in her eyes.

Argus gulped down a ball of spit forming in the back of his throat, pulling his eyes away from Lillian. "I did not come to Hawkhurst to banter with old friends, Lord Syomin." The title of Lord toward his old employer was habitual. It was unnecessary for him to address the man in such a way but Syomin did stand a bit straighter. Argus continued, "I was completing a job and was deceived. I am now in servitude to House Oenus."

"Interesting dilemma," Syomin gleamed. His smile was difficult to discern, only noted by a slight elevation of cheekbones and a turn at the corner of his tightened, thin lips. "So, you are the sellsword who is supposed to return Lillian to her father? Safe and sound, is it?"

"Something like that, yes." Argus straightened, the chair creaking once more underneath him. He ignored it, picturing the severed finger Lord Oenus had received from the *Bracken and Pine*. The mysterious letter had indicated Lillian was being tortured and cut to pieces. "I see all of her extremities are fully intact."

Syomin raised his eyebrows. "So, you have seen the letter then? Lord Oenus was unwise to show off that little piece of parchment. Things will be worse for him now."

Argus settled his hands across his lap to maintain his balance. "Should I think you sent the letter to Lord Oenus?"

"No," Syomin said. "House Ekdal would not do anything so bold."

"I too would have thought it was a bit daring even for thieves. Though, you must have some role in her disappearance given that she is here with you. Who is threatening Lord Oenus?" Argus asked.

"Why the genuine interest, Haakan? Your own house is at odds with Oenus. You would think you would want the same thing we want."

"It would be a fool's notion to think I have any care

what happens to House Madrin." Argus scowled.

"Ah, yes. You are a dishonorable man, Haakan. It was you who tried to murder his own mother." Syomin laced his words with venom.

Argus nearly fell out of the chair. "Tried?"

Syomin mocked him. "Did you not know she survived your attempt to kill her?"

Haakan Madrin!

He looked away from Syomin only to meet Lillian's eyes. The sadness within them was unbearable. Guilt pulsed against his innards.

Argus swallowed hard, changing the topic. "Who sent the letter to Lord Oenus?"

He wanted out of this blasted city as quickly as possible. He had more people recognizing him than not, and knowing his mother had survived his attack only made his presence in Hawkhurst more dangerous.

"That is not information for me to give. You should know better—"

Argus interrupted, molding his grief into fury, every word a dagger flung from his throat. "Why did you bring me here? You are not going to allow me to return Lillian to her house."

"Heavens, no! I would never allow that, Haakan," Syomin said. This time the smile was more evident on the man's thin face.

Syomin was digging under his skin in the way all thieves did. The bastards were trained to destroy a man's sense of peace. They truly stole everything they could manage to take.

Argus was quick to interrupt the laughter. "Then why have me brought here?"

"The *Eadfel*, Haakan. You should be well enough

aware that everything in this grand city has to do with the *Eadfel.*"

Telling Argus this had to do with the political games, or the *Eadfel*, really did not tell him anything at all. The thief might as well tell him oceans were made up of water.

"I would prefer if we do not talk in riddles. I have been on the surface for fifteen years. I do not have the energy or the patience to talk in circles." Argus did not blink.

Syomin softened his face. He referred to the surface people in his response. "The *Kedewin* have made you weak. I told you this would happen when you left. You did not listen to me. You could have gained your freedom from the Arena and worked towards obtaining a seat in House Madrin or House Sybaris, but instead you fled to your Uncle's house in Hawe."

"I don't need a lecture on my life, my bloodline, or the choices I have made," Argus said. He redirected the conversation back again. "Why did the hunters attack me on the streets?"

Haakan Madrin.

The sound of his old name echoed in his head as though it were being yelled from the stands of the Arena, the battlefield of the gladiators. He was not a gladiator anymore. That was in the past.

Syomin handed his last segment of armor to Lillian, who continued to remain silent with her large brown eyes watching all that transpired. He finally answered, "There are many in Middle City who would like to see House Quist come to ruin. With House Oenus rising in power, and with so much at stake, it is expected that Lord Oenus would have retaliated against the threats of House Quist upon receiving the letter threatening Lillian. No one expected the man to send for a sellsword."

Argus tugged at his memory. "The *Hunter's Guild* is run by Lord Garnoc from House Hedlund. But, last I knew, they hold more power than House Quist anyway."

"You are clever and remember much." Syomin dipped his head in recognition. "You know more than you give away."

"So, what is the current pecking order of the houses in Middle City?"

Syomin counted off on his fingers. "Oenus, Madrin, Etha, Hedlund, Quist, and Bloch."

Argus started to fit the pieces together.

"You are trying to advance your own house out of Lower City and into Middle City by eliminating a House. That is why you are helping." Argus reasoned, the chair nearly slipping out from underneath him as he shifted forward.

Lord Syomin breathed out of his nose, giving away what he likely did not want to say.

Argus stood up from the chair edging towards the desk that separated them.

"Why don't you target House Bloch?" Argus asked. "They are the weakest."

It was Lillian who responded. Her words were quick, holding little resemblance to the elegant tone of her father. "Because House Quist is the only remaining ally of my father's house in Middle City. If he does make it to Upper City, it will be short-lived without the support of the middle Houses."

Argus rubbed his fingers together, leaning against the desk with his free hand. It kept him from pacing around the room needlessly. The tables had turned and he had the advantage.

"Tell me, *Lady Oenus*, why would you want to aid in your father's downfall?"

She blinked a couple times, jaw angled as she forced the words from her lips. "He planned to marry me to Frederick Quist."

"And?"

"I love another."

"Of course you do." He muttered.

The plot was so thick that his head was spinning. This was exactly the reason why he did not dabble in the *Eadfel*. Every noble and their child were scheming to have their own wants satisfied. *'Greed was the bloodiest path to governance.'*

"Why don't we cut to the chase?" Argus continued. "What is it you are asking from me? As I told you in Middle City, I am well aware nothing is free in Hawkhurst."

Lillian shifted her eyes to Syomin, talking softly as though the walls had ears. "Lead my father to believe the evidence points toward House Quist. That is all. Be certain he does not suspect the Hedlunds or the Ekdals."

"And, what will I receive in return?"

"Your freedom, of course," Syomin said.

Argus laughed. "You cannot promise me that. No man has the power to give another man freedom."

"I got you out of the city once, Haakan. I can do it again."

Argus frowned. "I would ask for something more

immediate, Lord Syomin."

The man lifted his cheekbones again in amusement. "Looks like you are playing the *Eadfel* after all."

Argus ignored him. "Lady Lancaster needs to be freed from the Ascension and returned to her home in Galoroth."

It was Lillian's turn to laugh out loud. "That alone is a far more difficult task than what we are asking from you. Lying to a man is much different than freeing a person from the Ascension."

Syomin raised his hand to silence her. "We will look into what can be done. Is that all?"

"There is a gladiator from the Arena I need to have freed."

Lillian scoffed. "There are plenty of people captive in Hawkhurst. We cannot free everyone."

Syomin dropped his jaw in surprise. "What is her name?"

Argus said, "Karine the Swift."

Syomin's jaw dropped a bit more.

"It is important for me to maintain my position while in the city," Argus explained.

Syomin nodded. "I might be able to give you the opportunity to set her free, if you don't mind getting your hands a little dirty."

"It should not be too difficult. House Ekdal oversees the Arena and the gladiators," Argus argued.

"It is a bit more difficult than that," Syomin said. "Anything more?"

Argus ground his teeth in frustration before giving his final demand. "Stop calling me Haakan. My name is Argus Gunther."

Chapter 7

It was evening when Argus finally stepped outside the doors of the *Hand of Tear'n* and into the street near the center of Lower City. Since Hawkhurst was beneath the surface, there was no sun to determine the time of day. Instead, time was measured by the clanging of clocks in each district. The clock chimed seven times, marking evening, before it ceased.

With the final clang, an invigorated crowed roared in the distance. Argus knew the noise all too well. A crowd had gathered at the Arena down the street. He remembered the sound being much louder than what he heard, but it was a familiar tone.

Before he knew it, he found his feet treading toward the fighting pit. Despite what had been said in the *Hand of Tear'n*, the only thing pressing on his mind was that his mother was still alive.

He should have slit her throat instead of running her through with his sword. Years of agony suddenly flooded back. The woman deserved to die! She had abandoned him to a life of blood and death. Veina Sybaris was a whore worthy of nothing but death.

As for his father, Rotrderd Madrin, he would get

his soon enough.

Argus pulled the handkerchief from his chin up and covered his nose. He could not be too careful now that he knew both of his parents were alive. Either of them would be pleased to see him skinned in the streets.

The skin on the top of his scalp itched, telling him his red hair was trying to grow back. He had shaved it to hide his affiliation with the two families, but it seemed everyone was identifying him anyway. He knew being in Lower City and near the Arena increased the chances of more people recognizing him. It had once been his primary playground.

As he neared, he came to the realization he had never been a spectator at the Arena.

"Split her open!" A man applauded near the perimeter of the Arena. Folks around him cheered or booed in appreciation of his words. Many more yelled at the gladiators below.

"Kill him!"

"Keep an eye on that axe!"

The din of the crowd was deafening as they hooted and hollered. Argus squeezed through a pair of men to get a better view of the fighting beneath. Part of him grew curious as to whether his mother or father would be attending the fights.

The Arena was not immaculate in size when compared to the rest of the city. It was an oval imprint beneath the stands. Broken rocks and thick sands filled the belly, where the gladiators warred with one another. Around the edges of the half-moon dip were the benches carved from stones with stairs that led halfway down. One side was decorated with colored flags of the Houses of Middle City and Upper City, where the nobles would come and sit if they had time to enjoy the fights.

Today, there were no nobles to be found. In fact, the stands were relatively empty of spectators. Far emptier than when Argus used to battle below.

It did not take long before he was able to grab a seat and watch the gladiators beneath him. A man and woman clashed repeatedly, their weapons continuing to clang and echo against the partially empty stands.

The man was not an intimidating man. He was smaller than Argus, wielding an axe and shield against the lithe woman's single, thin sword. She was much more agile than the man. The woman parried and thrust, parried and thrust, to no avail against her stout opponent. The man simply blocked her attacks, focusing on his defense and waiting for an opening between her quick movements.

"Karine! Karine!" A patron shouted from behind Argus with a few others echoing the cheers.

Argus leaned forward a bit more with interest, checking that his handkerchief was well placed. This woman was Karine the Swift, the sister of Tolliver Wolfram, who he had met with earlier that afternoon.

He cringed, considering Tolliver knew he really was Haakan Madrin. Argus could not trust the stand-in owner of the *Bracken and Pine*. In his trade, Tolliver had the right connections, knowing all the prominent families in Hawkhurst, which meant the worm could make Argus's life more than difficult. Since Lady Astrid Lancaster had promised the man they would free his sister in exchange for his silence, Argus had little choice. Of course, Tolliver was also supposed to be telling Argus who had carried the letter to Lord

Oenus. But from the conversation with Syomin, Argus reasoned it was the Hedlund family.

There was always the possibility he could simply kill Tolliver. He imagined cutting through the yellow-skinned mage, who served as the warehouse operator's bodyguard, would be easier said than done. He simply hoped Syomin would free Karine and end this slight impasse.

"Karine, Karine! Karine, Karine!" The patrons behind him retorted again and again.

"Magar! Magar!" A few to Argus's left shouted louder, taunting the supporters, and giving praise to the other warrior.

Argus shifted in his seat. He remembered the feeling of hearing his name bellowed from the stands by supporters. It was uncanny but there was sense of belonging he had felt when hearing his own name shouted. It caused a man's blood to boil a bit hotter. It would give courage where it might have been lacking before.

The chanting increased in volume and cadence and Karine and Magar dueled with more ferocity.

Magar dug his heels into the sand, shield raised across his midsection and axe hanging against his thigh in a fist. Karine's sword was like a needle, piercing through the air high and low, but the man quickly blocked them. She spun to the right, dark locks twirling, and leapt into a roll. Her form was true as she plunged the weapon at Magar's midsection.

The man was ready. He twisted away, bringing the axe downward across the sword blade. The momentum ripped Karine's arm wide leaving her vulnerable. Because of his awkward stance, the man could not bring the axe back in time to strike the woman, or move his feet quick enough to close the distance to gain the advantage. Instead, his right arm released the shield and flung it towards the woman.

There was little to be done. The shield spiraled like a wagon wheel and smashed into the chest of the woman. Argus could hear her grunt, the air decompressing from her lungs. She landed on her back; her weapon fell from her reach.

Roars of excitement erupted on either side of Argus. Even from those who were so-called supporters of Karine the Swift.

Magar scrambled towards the fallen woman. His axe was lifted over his head with aim to crush her skull, but Karine had clearly gotten her nickname for reason. Although she could not breathe, she still had the sense to grab his shield in time to block the blow.

The man sneered, jerking his weapon back from the impact against the shield. He came down a second time, but this time, he sunk the axe into Karine's thigh lying beneath his spread feet.

The steel weapon split her flesh with ease. Karine bawled, her voice drowning out the sound of the crowd.

Argus stood with the several others around him.

Magar tried to pull the axe free but it was wedged into her femur. Her screams were drawn-out, tears flooding her vision, wetting the sands. Magar jerked at the weapon with desperation.

Suddenly, it was no longer an elated event to witness. People in the crowd cringed. The two gladiators were pinned against each other, faced with the reality of the pain they each inflicted on one another.

The cries of Karine silenced the crowd as she lay in torment, gripping the shield with both hands, while the opposing gladiator attempted to finish what he had started.

"Please…" Karine shuddered.

Argus gulped seeing the blood soaking into the sands.

"Take her sword and finish it already!" A man next to Argus cried out.

Magar acted as though the words were his own. He loosened his grip and searched for the needle sword in the sands. The man looked frantic, almost as though he was in as much pain as Karine herself.

Argus found the sword first, seeing the emblem of a broken sword imprinted on the handle of the blade. It was the work of the smithy at the *Rusty Blade*. Gladiators who were slaves were sponsored by nobles or businesses, while the free gladiators managed themselves. Karine's weapon indicated she was sponsored by the *Rusty Blade*. The shop would pay a handsome penalty if Karine died in the Arena.

Stepping down a row from where he had been sitting, Argus considered bolting for the weapon. He could not chance what Tolliver might do if Karine died.

Magar took two steps toward the weapon and then his head rocked left and right by some unseen force. The sickening crack of his neck snapping shocked the lot of them.

The crowd went berserk.

A woman cried out, "She is a sorceress! She killed him with magic."

"It is not allowed," another said.

"The Ascension will come. We must get out of here."

Argus stood from his seat with his own aim to get far from the gladiator pit. He could not get around the flailing crowd who argued among themselves.

"She could not have done it. She was barely conscious. Look at all the blood!"

"No, it was done by someone else, someone here in the stands."

"It does not matter. The Ascension will kill her anyway."

Argus found an opening and started moving up the stone steps towards the exit when he noticed the tall, yellow skinned man under heavy brown robes. The man's eyes flashed white.

Tolliver's henchman. Argus could not remember the bastard's name, but he knew him. The man had also started to pull at magic at the *Bracken and Pine*.

The henchman had to be the one who did this, but why were the mages from the Ascension not appearing as they had when Astrid cast magic in Middle City. They should be dragging the oversized man to their tower.

Argus paused, realizing the lackey was watching him. How long had he been following him?

The man was inconspicuous, dipping his head and turning towards the streets. He wanted Argus to follow him.

Against his better judgment, Argus obliged.

They walked by brothels, taverns, and churches in Lower City. The tall man did not stop, continuing beyond the *Crossroads*, toward Middle City. The henchman sauntered in a straight path giving little care or respect to anyone he passed. At first, Argus believed the man was going to take him back to the *Bracken and Pine* to meet with Tolliver, or even into an alley to finish the tussle they had started that morning. Though, the man did not begin to slow his pace until they were nearing *Creon's Inn*, where Argus was supposed to be staying with Astrid.

Argus cursed under his breath as they neared the place. Lord Oenus's House was right across the street, and would have eyes on him as soon as he entered the area if his spies hadn't already been watching him all day. But, the henchman did not go into the inn. Instead, he marched straight pass *Lady Sophia's Arms, Creon's Inn,* and through the front door of the *Rusty Blade*.

"Welcome, Abdul," Argus heard the smithy say as he followed the henchmen into the shop. That was the name! "She is being retrieved as we speak."

Argus received a gentle nod from the round smithy called Guddor Flan. The man barely looked at him a second time, allowing Argus to breathe a sigh of relief. The smithy had made him weapons and armor when he fought in the Arena years ago. Luckily, he did not recognize Argus.

Haakan Madrin.

This time the name in his head was shouted by the woman's voice he had heard when he first came to Hawkhurst. It was the sound of his mother, whom he had believed he had murdered before leaving the city.

He had been sure of it!

"Come this way, please," Abdul gestured, pulling an old blanket to the side at the rear of the shop. Argus could make out a faint, dimly lit room behind the makeshift curtain.

Argus shifted his weight uneasily but took the invitation into the separate room. He scanned the empty room. The room had a bedroll, some half-crafted pieces of weapons or armor, and a few crates and barrels. There was no table, no chair, and nothing of real significance.

He turned on Abdul the henchman. "What is this about?" Argus demanded.

"You have wasted time in freeing Karine, and now she has been injured because of your stupidity. You promised to set her free. How long do you wish for my master to keep your secrets?" Abdul whispered between tightened lips. His tone held more authority than Argus would have ever considered the man to have.

"Wasted time?" Argus breathed, eyes widening. "It has not even been a day!"

Abdul blew up his chest, stepping forward until their noses nearly touched. The sellsword held his ground. "It has been three."

"Three?" Argus laughed in Abdul's face. "Are you mad? I just spoke with you and Tolliver this morning."

An expression of uncertainty washed over Abdul momentarily before he squinted with a knowing look in his eye. "You really believe this?"

"You really believe the opposite? You must be mad. I am telling you the truth."

"I'm afraid it is only your version of the truth," Abdul said, stepping backwards. "You have been under a spell or some potion of sorts. Where did you go?"

Argus swallowed, feeling his fingers inching

together in attempts to lessen his anxiety. He did not trust Abdul any further than he could throw him. "That is not for you to worry about, Abdul."

Abdul opened his mouth to challenge the statement but was interrupted by two men coming through the curtain carrying an unconscious body.

Karine the Swift.

"Make way. She has lost a lot of blood," one of them said softly as though it were a secret she was there.

They laid her down carefully on the bedroll. Her skin was pale and lips parched. She looked far weaker in the small room than she had in the Arena.

The axe was still lodged into her thigh but the blood flow had slowed.

"Can you save her, Abdul?"

The tall man threw back his hood and nodded. "Of course. Go out front and keep watch."

Argus went to leave the room but was halted by Abdul.

"You, stay."

Argus shook his head. "I'll wait out front."

Argus could not measure how long he piddled in the storefront of the *Rusty Blade* trying to hide his features from the smithy. Fortunately, Gudder was mesmerized too much by his own work to worry about Argus. The man said he had an order needing filled by the end of the week and was not available for idle chitchat.

It was not long before the other shops had shut their shutters and locked their doors. The night grew thin in Hawkhurst. The district clocks clanged in the distance. Soon, the streets would be littered with nothing more than whores, thieves, and drunks.

Argus watched the sentries dim the lantern lights, signifying after hours had come in the subterranean city, when Abdul exited from the backroom with Karine the Swift. She hobbled lightly next to him, but the cut upon her leg was non-existent. Argus found that when the woman was not twisting her face in the shape of a woman wanting to kill another man—as she had in the Arena—she was a rather good looking girl. A small nose, thin lips, and round eyes decorated her face in a unique fashion.

"Her color looks much better than it had before," Gudder said. "It is good Tolliver has you to assist him, and Karine, of course."

Argus admitted the girl had some hue back in her cheeks. Though, with all the blood caked onto her skin, it was difficult to see the full of it.

"I do not need praise for the gifts the gods have given me," Abdul said. He turned his attention to the gladiator woman. "It will be sore for several days, so you are going to want to stay out of the Arena. Until then, try to make due in the Cogs."

Argus winced.

The Cogs were lower than Lower City in both physical location and prestige. It was a settling place for the poor, abused, or enslaved. Where Lower City housed those who were hardly worth any mention of status, the Cogs were inhabited by people who were hardly considered people at all.

"I cannot go to the Cogs, Abdul," Karine said. "You intervened with the battle. The authorities will blame me for Magar's bizarre death."

Abdul raised an eyebrow. "I think you will be safer

than you think. No one saw what I did."

Karine huffed, "I don't think the guard is going to care what you did. The man's neck was snapped without anyone touching him. I will be blamed for this."

Gudder dipped his head in agreement. "She has a point."

"Of course, I do. Too often fools think the guards have no brains. I cannot imagine what prompts such ignorance. They are trained in their trade as well as any other." She hobbled past Argus, eyeing him, and took a seat on a three-legged stool. "And, who are you?"

Argus took a step back at the intrusive tone. He nearly heard Tolliver's directness come through her voice.

"I am Argus Gunther of Hawe," he said, focusing on holding his feet to the floor. "Your brother asked me to free you from the gladiator pit." Argus was not sure why he told her as much, but the words had already fled from his lips before he could pull them back. He was becoming as loose-tongued as Astrid.

"That would be something." Karine scoffed. "My brother is always scheming some plan to free me from my bonds. He would do better to accept this as my lot in life."

"Do you want it to be?" Argus asked.

She turned her chin upward as though she were looking at him for the first time. The question was not meant to be as personal as it sounded, but it was clear the words had moved something within her. The edges of her eyes moistened.

Abdul pulled the hood of his robe back over his head, and moved to take Karine's hand. "Let's get you back to the Cogs."

"I told you I cannot return there. Even if the guards don't arrest me, the other slaves would kill me for breaking their unwritten code of combat."

Abdul grimaced. "You did not break the code. I did."

Karine said, "I am grateful for it, but you must understand what I am saying. There is nothing I could say without giving you up to the authorities. That would not please Tolliver."

"Still," Abdul said, "we cannot stay here. It is time to go. Argus will come with us to discuss the means to how he will free you."

Before Argus could argue with the arrogant man, the door behind him burst open. Three men in dark armor with steel in their hands scattered into the room, fanning wide.

"Karine Wolfram," a thicker man with a quivering chin said, "you are under arrest for misconduct in the Arena."

He looked around the room at Gudder, Abdul, and then Argus with hesitation.

A man held himself a bit straighter eyeballed Karine. He tightened his grip on the weapon. "I thought she was injured. There is a lot of blood, Wallace, but I don't see any wound."

"He is right, Captain," said the third.

"It does not matter," the thicker man said.

Karine stayed firmly planted on the chair. "I did not kill Magar...I do not know who did."

The Captain twitched but did not advance towards the gladiator. "All the same, you will do best to come with us. We do not want any trouble."

"Neither do we," Abdul interjected.

"You stay out of this," the third man said, "unless you want to join her at the *Ward*."

Abdul had an eerie smile. "I do not think anyone will be going to the *Ward* tonight, gentlemen. You would do best to leave here and rid your minds of the events of today."

The floorboards creaked as Gudder stepped away from the happenings in his shop. He scooted into the back room behind the curtain. Argus had a good mind to follow his example.

The Captain opened his mouth and then closed it again at Gudder's departure. It was the second man who filled the silence.

"It is only questioning. There is no reason to put anyone's life at risk."

"He is right," Karine said, springing up from her stool and stepping in front of Abdul.

"No!" Abdul growled.

"There is no other way. I will go willingly, if anything, to prove my innocence." Karine pushed back from Abdul, locking in with his gaze. Her steps were as light as duck feathers as she moved into the custody of the guards.

"Tell my brother I love him," she cooed to Abdul.

They pulled her back out from the *Rusty Blade*.

The tall man's eyes flashed white.

Chapter 8

Abdul sank back from the door, crestfallen. His hand twitched next to his side. Argus was unsure of the extent of the man's actual power, but it seemed as though he were about to unleash it on the guardsmen who had taken Karine.

"If you go after her, it will not end well for you...or her," Argus said.

"I know," Abdul rumbled. He stared with the door in disbelief, his eyes filled with hurt.

"I imagine this is not going to set well with Tolliver," Argus said with a hint of disdain, poking at the man. He could not stop the small smile from forming between his cheeks.

"You should be worried about that." Abdul sneered back.

"Me?" Argus laughed. "You are the one who intervened in the Arena. Your actions sentenced her to death. I did nothing."

"Exactly." Abdul clenched his fists at his side. "You are the one who has not fulfilled your promise. You were supposed to rescue her. If I had not saved her, your secret would have been released to all of

Hawkhurst."

"Quiet!" Argus hushed, darting his eyes to the back room where Gudder had gone.

"You should consider yourself dead already!" Abdul exclaimed.

Argus gulped, almost moving towards the door to go after the woman. "She will likely be burnt alive in the Skyway for this."

"We could only be so lucky. It is winter on the surface and the sun barely shines. She would not be taken until spring," Abdul predicted.

Argus rustled between his teeth. "What do you expect me to do? I cannot take on the entire Capsa Guard. I would be cut down long before I reached the *Ward*."

"You will find a way or all of Hawkhurst, including Oenus, will know you for who you really are. That information alone might be enough of a bargaining chip to set Karine free."

Argus stared hard at Abdul, knowing the warning held more truth than threat. Jimi Oenus's older sister was married to Lord Capsa, who controlled the guardsmen and supervised the *Ward*. The connections were well in place to ruin Argus.

Abdul adjusted his hood, maintaining his scornful countenance. "I am leaving. Tolliver needs to know what has happened."

Argus gritted his teeth. "Do not leave out any details about what brought this about."

"I intend to tell everything, as I always do." Abdul frowned. He stormed by Argus and into Middle City.

The door banged shut.

Argus stood there for only a few moments before

taking his leave from the *Rusty Blade*.

He only caught a glimpse of Abdul's hunkering figure hurrying away. The man was gone from sight in a matter of seconds. Argus sighed and headed next door to *Creon's Inn*.

He was walking up the steps when he heard his name.

"Argus, Darling! I thought you were dead."

Madame Maggie Halum stood near the entrance of the inn with her purplish veil pulled up around her red hair. Her full lips smacked with delight, looking him up and down.

He halted under her green eyes. '*The gaze of woman was as perplexing as life itself.*' "Not yet."

"You have been missing for several days. There are many in the city who have grown worried that you had escaped again. It would have been better if you had died then to attempt to flee."

Argus tensed his jaw, feeling eyes upon him. He looked around noticing only a few stragglers on the street. He found it was best not to get reeled in by her mind games. As his Uncle Peter would say, '*Idle chitchat is but a friendly interrogation. Batting eyes and kissy lips are also painted on the faces of wolves.*'

Seeing the Madame dressed up in her veil suddenly reminded Argus of the *Huntsman Tale*. It told of an axman, wiser than most, who was forced to tear through a wolf's belly to save a granny and some brat grandchild.

"What are you doing here?"

"Oh." Her nostrils flared with amusement. "I did not come looking for you, darling. Do not worry yourself. Business calls, you know?"

Argus grunted, which may have been relief. Then again, he was well aware that his mood was sour from the incident with Abdul. "Have a pleasant evening."

Madame Halum continued like he had not said a word. "You know, Vahka Etha has a terrible hunger for whores. Much to his father's dissatisfaction, he calls upon my ladies at *Feather Her Goose* more than any other noble. He is upstairs with one of them as we speak, emptying his youth."

Argus felt his stomach churn, quickly doing the math in his head. House Etha was one of the few houses in Middle City aligned with his father's house, House Madrin. House Etha was also one of the many houses in opposition to House Oenus "I don't know why you are telling me this. I am sure Lord Etha would not appreciate you sharing such things about his son."

She laughed. "It is hardly a secret. The entire town knows of his carnal affliction. I believe you met House Etha's courier, Thorin Awklee, a few days ago outside of the *Bracken and Pine.*"

He barely remembered the dark haired, dark-eyed boy. "Is there anything you do not know, Maggie?"

She smiled behind her veil. "No, I suppose not. Would you like to know more about dear Thorin?"

"I do not have the interest or the time. House Etha's affairs can stay private. I am not going to play the *Eadfel*," Argus said.

"You already are, Darling. Even after fifteen years, you know the layout and politics of this city as well as anyone else."

Argus clapped his hands together. "It tells you how much any of you really accomplish in your little games, doesn't it?"

The Madame grinned, green eyes sparkling. She changed the topic as footsteps fell behind Argus. "It could always be a better night. I could send Alys your way if you need some company. She did show some interest in you when you arrived with Lady Lancaster."

Argus stretched his memory, remembering the prostitute with creamed locks who had tried to seduce him by the steps of *Feather Her Goose*. "I am not interested."

"Mr. Gunther," a familiar, melodious voice resounded from behind him. "You will come with me."

"Lord Oenus." Madame Halum curtsied in acknowledgement. "A pleasure to see you out so late."

Argus slumped his shoulders in defeat and turned to face the Lord. The man wore a black cloak that shrouded his garments. The symbol of House Oenus, the golden winged pennant, was in the same place it had been the first time they had met, upon the Lord's left breast. The massive ornament of the blood moon, the symbol Cauthe, hung from his neck.

Jimi Oenus turned towards the Madame only momentarily, presenting himself much differently than he had at her establishment. "I do not need the tribute of a raunchy sprite, Madame. Run back to your rickety shack and keep your flea-bidden furrow away from my doorstep."

Argus's chin could not have dropped any lower, but Maggie stood in absolute calm.

She curtsied again. "Yes, my Lord. I was just leaving."

Argus did not have opportunity to watch the Madame disappear into the night. Instead, he turned his gaze to Lord Oenus and tried to tighten his blasted nose so it would not give away his bloodline. Lord Oenus must not know he was the child of Sybaris and Madrin. The crooked nose was going to be the death of him.

"Come," the Lord said again. Jimi turned on his heel and strode towards his large estate across the street.

The two of them passed through the black iron gates, set between iron fences, and guarded by the Capsa Guard. The building was three times the size of *Creon's Inn*, and spoke of a long-lasting dynasty in Middle City. Argus was not certain how long House Oenus had been in a top-ranking house, but it was before Argus had been born.

Argus tried to take in the setting and the astonishing pleasantries that made up the Oenus estate, but his eyes were fixated on something else entirely. The master-crafted lute on the back of Lord Oenus bounced softly with each step. The wood, strings, and engravings on the musical instrument were mesmerizing, perfectly chiseled into the wood. It must have been crafted by magic. It was far more interesting than anything the estate had to offer.

It was not until they had passed through the double-doored entryway, through the foyer, and into a sitting room that Argus fully to realized he was within the walls of the Oenus home.

He might as well be walking into the lion's den.

"Have a seat." Jimi motioned towards a cushioned seat across from a desk chiseled from some sort of gem. The entirety of the desk was sapphire in color, with a yellowish light that glimmered within its holdings. The light was hypnotic, ricocheting within the confines of the stone.

Argus sat easily on the chair, somewhat pleased when it did not creak in the slightest. It was much more comfortable than the dilapidated seat that Syomin Ekdal had offered him in the *Hand of Tear'n*.

Lord Oenus unstrapped his lute and leaned it against the desk.

"I believe an explanation is in order, Mr. Gunther. You have tried my patience. Where have you been for the past few days?"

Argus relaxed. Lord Oenus was not as informed as he had assumed.

"I have been doing as you instructed, my Lord. I was investigating your missing daughter and the letter you had received from House Quist." Argus was surprised at how calm his voice was when responding to the imposing man.

"Have you?" Jimi Oenus questioned, clicking his tongue. He pulled off the Cauthe emblem and removed his black cloak. His dress was expressive with gold and blue, and niches of plum. The colors lightened Lord Oenus's blue eyes, causing them to shine nearly as bright as the desk.

"Yes, my Lord," Argus said. He tried to be quick in his responses. The man should not have any reason to think him to be lying, and in truth, he was being honest thus far. But, he knew what question was coming, and he was going to have to make a choice.

"And what have you found, Mr. Gunther?"

Argus's mouth went dry. That was the exact question he would have preferred to put off until he had more time to think. His options were to tell Lord Oenus about Syomin Ekdal and Lillian, to place blame on House Quist, or to lie altogether.

"Jimi?" A woman's shoes clicked across the floor from the rear. "Who is here?"

Argus welcomed the interruption, turning to face the dark-haired woman in her evening gown.

Jimi stood, motioning for Argus to do the same. "Mr. Gunther, my wife, Armine, daughter of the belated Mirac Hedlund."

Argus nearly tripped over his own feet in attempts to stand. He luckily found the grace to bow formally before lifting his eyes back to the man's wife. Armine Hedlund? Lord Oenus was married to the sister of the very men who were trying to destroy him.

She dipped her head in return. Her annoyed expression did not match her polite gesture. "Well met, Mr. Gunther."

"Likewise, my Lady."

Armine hummed in recognition and then addressed her husband. "Isn't it a bit late to be having business meetings, Darling?"

"We will not be long, Armine. I promise."

She lifted an eyebrow. "I have heard that one before. Please lock up when you are finished. I am heading to bed."

"Yes, Dear. Of course."

Argus noticed Lord Oenus take a slow breath as his wife made her exit. The interruption may have caused him to recognize his own haste in the discussion. From what Argus could tell, it was not typical of the man to rush his words.

"You were saying – about what you have discovered about my daughter?"

Argus eased himself back into his seat. Time was up. "Lillian's disappearance seems to be pointed towards House Quist. I have not discovered any other leads, my Lord."

"No!" Jimi yelled.

Argus shifted against the chair, taken aback by the explosive response.

"That cannot be. What have you done to look into this?" Jimi's knuckles were white against his desktop, hands balled into fists. Argus must have appeared quite perplexed, because he gave some explanation. "House Quist has no reason to steal away my daughter or to send me threats. Aaron Quist is my only ally in Middle City and his son, Frederick, is to wed Lillian in a month's time. Listen, someone has done well in staging this little act, and covering up their trail. I refuse to think Aaron is behind this."

Argus felt his eyebrow quiver, and he suddenly focused on tightening up his nose again to take his mind off the rest of his body. "Does Frederick have a genuine interest in marrying your daughter, my Lord?"

Jimi tilted his chin. "I do not see how that is a significant question. It does not matter what the man wants. The arrangement is set between Aaron and myself. Their house has everything to gain."

"I understand, my Lord," Argus said. He tried to find a tactful, well-measured way to lay out his case. "Though, it could be that a child, perhaps Frederick, is directing this charade and not Lord Quist himself."

"He would have my daughter in time."

Argus had hoped Jimi would have made up a motivation for House Quist instead of him having to create one. "I cannot imagine what would prompt such an act unless Frederick is in love with another. I am but a simple man."

"From Hawe?" Lord Oenus lifted an eyebrow.

"Yes, my Lord." Argus shifted in his seat.

"You will investigate this potential love interest of Frederick and see if the theory holds any water. I will be meeting with Lord Quist in the morning to discuss the letter." Jimi finally turned away from Argus, softening his gaze and paced behind his desk.

Argus tried not to watch the man, and directed his attention to the room. Some paintings of tavern life hung from the walls, depicting drinking patrons, barmaids, and bards singing or telling stories. Many of the storytellers held lutes like that of Lord Oenus. In fact, at closer inspection, it appeared to be the same lute.

"Are we understood?"

"Yes, my Lord," Argus said. He was not equipped to play the *Eadfel*, and he doubted this was a lie he could maintain for long. But, Syomin had helped him escape the city once. He could not imagine Lord Oenus having the same integrity.

The world had truly gone sour when he trusted a thief over a politician.

"I am aware of the *little* incident in Middle City and that Lady Lancaster has been taken to the Ascension. Tell me, what exactly happened?" The man peered over his shoulder casually. Lord Oenus was erratic, emotionally charged in one moment and calm the next. He might as well be a drunk man coming out of a tavern after a long night of debauchery.

Argus pulled at his Uncle Peter's advice, *'Questions are like bait dangling over an inescapable snare. Unless you fancy being peg-legged, answer with questions or not at all.'* "I was hoping you could shed some light on the issue. The entire incident took us both by surprise."

Lord Oenus chuckled. "You are either incredibly smart, Mr. Gunther, or incredibly stupid. You dance as well as that sultry whore you were speaking with earlier tonight."

Argus pressed his fingers together. The middle of his back twitched much like it once did before stepping into the gladiator pits. He cared little whether Lord Oenus spoke poorly of Maggie, but the man was so subtle in his threats that Argus could not determine if the man *actually* knew something or if he was just prodding for information.

'Poison the entire barrel of ale and pray your enemy orders a drink.'

"You have nothing to say, Mr. Gunther?"

"It seems difficult to complete the task without Lady Lancaster, my Lord. She knows the ways of nobles better than I."

"I get the impression you are not enthused to perform the duties Kern has retained you to complete." Lord Oenus half-smiled.

The thought of Landon Kern, his so-called employer, who had tricked him into serving House Oenus did not bring warm feelings to Argus. The man had sold Argus into slavery to erase his debts.

He was determined not to let Lord Oenus know how much hearing Kern's name disturbed him.

Argus shrugged, attempting to maintain his poise and meekness. He kept his voice low-slung. "My apologies, my Lord. I want to go home. I am a sellsword, not a guardsmen nor investigator. I do not have the skillset to find your daughter."

The words alone could get him killed. '*A useless man is not really a man at all.*'

"You are a sellsword." Jimi scoffed, lifting his lute from its sitting place. "You are whatever you are paid to be."

"Doesn't make me good at it."

Jimi strummed the lute. The sound was suave and sweet, a melody which Argus had never heard. He sunk into the chair feeling numb and lightheaded. It was as though the sound was surging through his veins as smoothly as his blood.

Jimi hummed with the tune. "Mr. Gunther…Mr. Gunther…"

The man's voice faded with the music.

"Wha—" Argus struggled to keep his eyes open. The room spun as his eyelids drooped and closed.

He was certain his body had completely fallen asleep when a small tremor, like a shockwave, pulsed against his temples.

"Mr. Gunther…"

The music was spellbinding, flowing from one key to the next as though it were a honeyed lullaby sung to children who were feigning off night terrors. Argus fought against the enchantment, his energy draining.

Haakan!

Chapter 9

"Vrorgard was one of the finest gladiators who had ever fought in the Arena," a gruff voice roused Argus from his slumber. "I remember the day he came limping out into the sand with his old wounds scabbed over and lips chapped from dehydration. The man could barely stand but the crowds screamed for him all the same."

Argus groaned, head aching like he had been hit with the hilt of a sword. The man's words sounded garbled against his eardrums. He tried to sit up, but he could not even open his eyes.

"Before his last fight, the Capsa Guard had him under the Skyway, scorching and burning for two days, you know? His feet were swollen and cut, brimming with pus and infection. Some people said he had gotten the Rot and was going to die anyway. Though, the fans knew Vrorgard was a good man and would rather die in battle then in a dirty cell."

"Why are you telling me this?" Argus managed to choke out of his parched throat. His eyes were as heavy as iron mail.

The speaker snorted and continued, "The

Hawkhurst god, Cauthe, did not look pleasantly on Vrorgard. It may have been the man's worship of the Sun God that drew him to madness. Then again, before he was enslaved, his father and mother had been slaughtered for squandering away riches from Upper City folks. That would make any man lose his mind."

There was a brief pause.

"The Crier told the crowd that Vrorgard would try to protect himself against three feral beasts from the surface. Maned, ferocious creatures with the biggest teeth and claws a man had ever known. It was going to be the most impressive battle of the century, so the Crier said."

Argus forced his eyes open with what energy he could muster. The innkeeper, the gladiator, and the apparent storyteller – Creon Nass – sat next to his bedside drying a mug with a hand towel. It may have been the same mug Argus had seen the man with days ago.

It was definitely the same beady, gloomy eyes staring at him.

"The Upper and Middle Houses sat on their benches under their flags, drinking their wine and wiping their crumbs from embellished robes, watching this man who prepared himself to die for nothing but the entertainment of moneyed men. Vrorgard could not be their pawn any longer."

"He killed himself," Argus said. Creon waggled his head, tensing his right arm, covered in banded armor.

"You have heard the story," Creon said. "Then you know Vrorgard put his sword through his own chest."

Argus grunted. It was unwise for him to admit to know any story from Hawkhurst.

Creon stood from the stool, the half-crescent moon axe shifting in his leather belt.

"Why share this story, Creon?"

"Gods have their flocks, rich men have their riches, gladiators have their audiences, but it is few men who ever find freedom."

Argus tried to sit up. "You are telling me to kill myself?"

"Nay, I would never propose that a man take his own life." He continued to scrub the mug. "Though there are some things worse than death."

"How did I get here?" Argus asked.

"I brought you here, of course, Mr. Gunther." Creon made his way to the door. "Lord Oenus had a message to give you. Said you best set your feet on a path forward and stop stalling."

Argus frowned. "I have hardly been stalling."

Creon shrugged. "You also have a visitor. He has been waiting in the tavern for half a day for you to wake. I will send him up."

"Half a day?"

"Hmm," Creon droned, dipping his head towards the window. It was nightfall again.

"Who is it?" Argus asked.

Creon attempted to keep his face calm, but there was a noticeable glint in his eye. "Sobrinos Bloch."

The innkeeper left the room and Argus stiffened, twisting his neck just enough to take in the miniscule window to the right of the bed. There was no feasible way he was going to be able to leap through that hole in the wall unless he sawed off his legs first.

"Sobrinos, you relentless cur," he said with disbelief. Argus swung his legs over the edge of the bed carefully and stood, wobbly on his feet.

He had been recognized by several people within the city, but this threatened everything. Sobrinos was his cousin, a son of Lord Sath Bloch and his father's sister. Although Argus was estranged from the family, Sobrinos knew him well.

The door opened without any knocking. Sobrinos was dressed in dark reds with black stitching. In fifteen years, the man had noticeably aged with gray filling his goatee and sprinkled through his shortened dark hair atop his head. He carried himself with an air of confidence, back stiffened and chin upright. He had the demeanor and look of his father more than his mother. He looked more like a Bloch than a Madrin.

"Haakan, Cousin." Sobrinos enlarged his chest, lifting his arms in greeting. "Welcome back. How have you been?"

Argus did not budge from his sitting position. "How did you find me, Sobrinos?"

"That is a silly question." Sobrinos chuckled, lowering his arms from their extension. He stepped softly around the room to face Argus. Though, he chose to stand instead of taking the stool that Creon had sat upon.

"How did you find me?" Argus repeated.

Sobrinos pushed air out of his nose, dispersing his smile. "You are resting in the inn adjacent to my mother's shop. It was really only a matter of time before you were recognized."

Argus hung his head. Of course! *Lady Sophia's Arms* was managed by Sophia Bloch, maiden name Madrin, his father's sister. Sobrinos would frequent the area.

"It was one of the smithy's there named Zankul who gave your description to me. I had been on an errand to fetch him silver ore to create some piece of armor for the Sybaris House. Never mind that. You should be lucky I am the one who has found you."

"Why is that?"

The smile returned to Sobrinos face in response to the question. "Certainly, you are not back in Hawkhurst to make peace with your family, Haakan. I mean, you did try to kill your own mother. I would not say House Sybaris or Madrin would be too forgiving if they found you. Not to mention, your father lost a lot of money when you escaped the gladiator pits."

"It is about the money then?" Argus should not have been surprised. Killing his mother, or trying to, had been one of the hardest things he had ever attempted to do. It haunted him daily. But, his father only cared about the money.

Sobrinos shrugged. "People die. Money does not."

"Let us cut to the chase," Argus said, not finding the reason to get into a philosophical battle with the man. "Why did you come to see me?"

"You are family, of course," Sobrinos said.

Argus was quick to respond. "That contradicts your *people die, and money doesn't* speech. Don't you think?"

Again, Sobrinos shrugged, his red robes rising and falling. "I wanted to know why you were in Hawkhurst."

It was likely the most straightforward statement Argus had heard from any man in the city. "And, you thought I would just tell you?"

"It has been many years, Haakan. But, if you recall,

I have never betrayed you." Sobrinos lifted his hands, palms open. "What can I say? Prying into the lives of others is my forte and curiosity has gotten the better of me."

Argus put his hands on his knees, pressing downwards. He needed more help if he was going to get out of the city alive. At this point, he did not know whom he could trust. The most he could consider was to rely on old bonds to see him through the storm.

"I had a contract to deliver a young lass to Lord Oenus. When I delivered her, I found out I was also part of the deal." Argus felt his anxiety tripping up, and pressed his fingers together gently. His hands were starting to shake. He did not know what Jimi Oenus had done to him, but he felt more on edge than usual. "Oenus has promised my freedom after I have done some things for him."

"Continue," Sobrinos encouraged.

Argus lifted his gaze to the man, hardly noticing he had been staring at the floor while speaking. "It has nothing to do with House Madrin or House Bloch, but it has gotten me in some trouble."

"Like what?"

"The lass has been taken to the Ascension."

Sobrinos widened his eyes. "She is a mage then."

Argus grunted. "But that is not the whole of it. I also have promised a man I would free his sister from the pits, and she has been taken to the *Ward*."

"Karine Wolfram," Sobrinos nodded. "I heard about her arrest early this morning. Tolliver is more dangerous than he appears. He has many unique relationships throughout the city. His position gives him authority in name, but not necessarily in practice."

"I am going to have to break her out of the *Ward*, or he will tell others who I am," Argus said.

"Ah," Sobrinos clasped his hands together, his cheekbones rising in amusement, "Lord Oenus does not know you are Haakan Madrin."

Argus nearly laughed out loud, and not because it was funny, but because he was not sure what other emotion to display. "I don't know what Lord Oenus knows, to tell you the truth. He refers to me by the name I gave him, Argus Gunther of Hawe, but his actions suggest he is on to me."

"He is not a dull man, but any measure," Sobrinos agreed. "So, you have to rescue a girl from the mages and another from the guards? Sounds like you need some practice with managing the damsels."

"I am not in the mood for your jokes," Argus said, holding back the grin pulling at the corners of his mouth.

"What help do you need, Haakan?" Sobrinos asked.

Argus found his strength had come back, and he stood from the bed. "I cannot owe any man any more. I am not gifted in the *Eadfel*, Sobrinos. I will start to lose my mind if I have to remember another task needing to be done. I am a fighter, not a thinker."

"Let me think for you then," Sobrinos offered, taking a step back to let Argus by him. Argus discovered his sword and handkerchief lying under the windowsill. "I am not asking for anything in return."

"Nothing is free in Hawkhurst."

Sobrinos was genuine. "Trust me, Cousin."

Chapter 10

A week had passed since Argus had come through Hawkhurst's front gates. Now that he was nearing them once more, his chest tightened in thinking about how nothing was going as planned. He was supposed to be in and out. Instead, he was traipsing through the streets of Upper City without any control over his own destiny.

The feeling was too familiar to him. He swallowed vomit.

Citizens and guardsmen stirred in the streets, making their way back home or to their designated posts.

"Slow down. You are going to bring too much attention to us, Argus."

The sound of Abdul's voice anchored Argus into reality and he slowed his pace. He could not hear the soft footsteps of Abdul or Sobrinos funneling behind him, but their yammering had kept him well aware of their presence.

"Are you sure you made the necessary arrangements?" Abdul probed Sobrinos behind him.

Sobrinos sighed beneath a black hood, which he

had worn for this certain occasion, keeping his identity well hidden. He spoke with an accent that Argus barely understood. "Told chou the guard hay been brib'd and the rear door was open'd fer us. Stop pesterin' me, eh? Chou will see when chou see."

Argus stifled his groan. Sobrinos was a gifted man, but the accent was overkill. Last night, he and Sobrinos had structured a plan to rescue Karine, and hopefully, get Tolliver and Abdul off his back. It had not been difficult to convince Tolliver to have his lackey join them on this venture. Argus had visited with them at the *Bracken and Pine*, and shared with them that he had found friends to help rescue Karine. Their agreement was nearly instantaneous.

Abdul grumbled under his own brown hood. "We look like a troupe of bandits walking down the street this way with our faces hidden and our weapons concealed."

"Chou ain't holdin' a weapon."

Argus sniffed, talking over his shoulder. "I don't see any other options, Abdul. If we are recognized, we will be dead by tomorrow morning. Now, keep quiet, both of you."

There was no argument as the three of them exited the Veii District and into the Sybaris District, the residence of Argus's mother's family. They strolled by the *Weary Squire Inn* and within sight of the *Scarlet Forge*.

Argus's finger and thumb found each other as they continued down the cobblestone. Lord Gargyan Sybaris, his uncle, was standing out front speaking with another man rather boisterously. The manager of the forge was nearly identical to Argus with a large red beard and shaven head. The sellsword turned his head from the scene, adjusting his handkerchief to cover his own beard.

He pondered whether his mother was inside the forge. Living. Breathing.

His back was tingling, muscles flexing, by the time they made it to the Capsa District. They crossed in front of the *Hawkhurst Barracks*, ignoring the guards who ignored them.

"The *Ward* is right up 'head," Sobrinos said. "Chou ain't goin' to want to be on the streets. Chou hay to head down the alley an' to the back."

Argus grunted, hanging a quick right between the two buildings. His hand itched to grip the hilt of his sword at his belt, but he maintained his composure. He did not need to draw unwanted attention when they were so close.

The rear door to the *Ward* stood ajar up ahead with a single man standing in front of it.

"I thought you said it was going to be left unattended," Abdul mumbled.

"That is me contact, Gero Pagdorf. Chou don't need to be worrin', eh? He will have it all spick an' spack."

It was all Argus could do not to shake his head at his cousin's nonsense. He had no idea what the man was talking about. *Spick and spack?*

Gero was alert, noticing the three of them advancing as soon as they turned the corner on the backside of the iron-cased building. He casually rocked on his heels, monitoring the back alleyway, rustling his dark beard while he waited for them to close the distance.

When they were within whispering distance, Gero said, "Don't say a word. None of you. I don't want to know who you are or what this is all about. The woman you are looking for is through this door. You take your first left, then your second right, and you will find her behind an iron door. It unlocks with this key, which you will bring back to me."

Gero offered the key to Argus, who took it gently from the man's outstretched hand.

The guard continued, "If you know anything, you know I am an officer of the *Ward*. For tonight, though, you do not know me anymore than I know you. The agreement is that you take your woman—nobody else—and you will not kill any of the guardsmen."

Argus nodded in acknowledgement.

"Get along," Gero ordered, jerking his head away to watch the alley again.

Argus sifted through the doorway into a hazy hallway. On tiptoes, he crept forward to make room for Abdul and Sobrinos to scoot into the corridor behind him. A few lanterns had been extinguished, causing it to be darker than it should have been.

"Gero ain't takin' chances. Keep to the darkness an' move with haste," Sobrinos said with his absurd twang.

"Why don't you take the lead, Sobrinos?" Abdul suggested. "You are smaller than the two of us."

Silence filled the passageway.

Argus peered over his shoulder where Sobrinos glared daggers at Abdul.

His flabbergasted cousin finally forced the words from his lips. "You know it is me?"

"Huh? Yes–of course. Why wouldn't I know you?"

"Just how?"

Abdul shrugged. Even cloaked in robes, it was obvious the yellow-skinned man was befuddled. His tone was waterless. "I am a mage, Sobrinos."

Sobrinos threw back his hood with the temperament of a harlot who just provided service to a penniless merchant. "Why in Cauthe's name have I been using this ridiculous accent, then?"

Abdul turned to Argus as though he might provide help. When none was offered, he turned back to Sobrinos and scrunched his shoulders.

Sobrinos kicked at the floor, finding a loss for words. "Cauthe-dammit."

"Perfect," Argus muddled. "Can we continue?"

An arrow zinged by Abdul's head and clanged against the iron door on the opposite side. A second one struck the man in the bicep, tearing through the full of the arm and into the side of his chest.

Abdul cried out, slinking back into the wall near the iron door they had entered.

Argus did not have the time or space to draw his sword. He rotated and face the two guards who were each nocking another arrow.

With a burrowed growl, Argus rushed them. The first bowman dropped his weapon and pulled a curved sword from his belt while moving toward the three. He was not as fast as Argus, who met him head-on. Argus grabbed the man's sword hand just as he pulled the blade from its sheath. With his free hand, Argus grabbed the man by the neck and flung him into the iron wall.

The clang of the man's dark armor against the wall echoed. Another arrow tore down the corridor. Argus did not have the time to see if it struck anything worthwhile. He focused on the enemy in his hands and slammed him into the wall again.

The guard slackened his grip on the sword. Argus let go of the man's neck and struck him in the elbow. The sellsword was a whirlwind, a flash of lightning; Argus was born for battle. He caught the sword by the hilt as it fell and pushed the guardsman sideways as another arrow rushed down the hallway. The arrow tore through the back of the man's neck. He gurgled and tumbled into a heap against the opposite wall.

The bowman froze in shock. By the time the curved sword gyrated over the length of the passage and sunk into the man's face, right between the nostrils and upper lip, he still had not reacted.

"Haak…Argus!" Sobrinos fizzled. "We weren't supposed to kill anybody."

"Is he going to be okay?" Argus heaved between deep breaths. He glanced at the door to the outside where Gero Pagdorf was stationed. The man either had not heard the ruckus or he did not care to know.

"You killed two guards in less than a minute."

"I know, Sobrinos. What about Abdul?"

Abdul pulled at the arrow in his arm and strained to hold back any sound. "I'll live…" He reached around with his right hand and snapped the fletching off the back of the shaft. With a jerk, he ascended his left arm and tore it free of the thin wood. The lingering piece remained in his side. "Help me up."

His voice was wheezing.

Sobrinos aided the man to his feet. "I think it pierced your lung. If it had been your heart, you'd already be dead."

Abdul coughed into his shoulder. "Don't...we will take care of it when we are done."

Argus nodded. "Let's go."

The sellsword led the way through the shadowy hallway with no immediate threats around the first corner. Sobrinos dawdled behind with Abdul. In truth, a deaf man would have heard Abdul panting. Argus could hear his Uncle Peter's voice cautioning him, *'the only sound more annoying than the chatter of a child is a mewling of a man.'*

Argus was not as light as Sobrinos would have been scrambling down the hallway, but he made his way well enough. He reached the second corner that they were meant to turn down and peeked around the corner. A lone guard stood outside the door holding Karine the Swift.

Argus lifted his finger to his lips and motioned for Sobrinos and Abdul to come closer. Upon seeing the guard, Sobrinos removed a dagger from beneath his cloak, but Abdul stopped him. Abdul lifted his hand towards the guard, eyes flashing white, and the guard dropped to the ground.

The jangle of him hitting the floor rung against the iron walls.

"Three dead!" Sobrinos exclaimed, standing upright. "Do you two not understand that this is my reputation here? There was an agreement that we're meant to adhere to, and you have killed *every* guard we have come across. I was going to knock him out with the dagger's hilt! The hilt!"

Abdul whispered, "I put...him to sleep. Not dead."

Sobrinos popped his head around the corner. The guard was snoring. "Oh."

Argus slapped his cousin on the shoulder and moved to the door. The door was solid iron. He stepped over the guard and fit the key into the lock.

He twisted it with ease, cracking the door. It grinded against the cobblestone floor. "Karine?"

"Who is that?" she answered.

Karine emerged from the darkness of the cell with her large, round eyes staring into his own.

Argus pulled the handkerchief down, his beard scratching his upper lip. "We have to go. Come on."

"Mr. Gunther. Is that you?"

Argus twisted on his heel to the door on the opposite side of the hallway.

"Astrid!"

"Mr. Gunther!"

Argus awkwardly pulled the key from the door.

"Karine, you are okay?" Abdul rasped, collapsing to one knee behind Argus.

"Abdul," Karine gasped, "you are hurt." She stumbled from the cell to embrace the man.

Argus disregarded the two of them, trying to press the key into the iron door holding Astrid.

"It doesn't fit." Argus slammed his hand against the iron. "What are you doing in the Ward?"

"Who is it?" Sobrinos asked, putting his hand to the iron door.

"Argus...please," she pleaded from the other side.

"It is Astrid Lancaster."

Sobrinos gulped. "Your other damsel. What are the chances?" He rubbed his chin thoughtfully. "The agreement was only to rescue one prisoner."

"We cannot leave her here," Argus said, tracing his hands along the edges of the door. There had to be some weakness. "Astrid, can you hear me?"

"Yes, Argus." Astrid sniffled from the other side. "Please…help me. Please."

Argus tugged at his beard. "Listen, Astrid. You are going to have to use your magic. Whatever you can do to open this door."

His words were followed by heaving sobbing, almost immediate, on the other side of the door. "I…cannot…Mr. Gunther. Those mages…dispelled me."

Sobrinos, as if finally making up his mind, turned to Abdul, seeing the clear answer. He pulled Karine from the man with a mild touch. "Open this door. Rip it from its hinges."

No more did his words leave his lips that a handful of crossbow bolts rained through the passage. Argus clung to the wall and Karine sprung back into her cell.

Abdul did not have a chance. Four arrows decorated his neck and chest. He keeled over with blood dribbling from his lips, eyes cold as hoarfrost.

Sobrinos took a bolt to the belly before collapsing to his side. As Abdul's corpse landed next to him, Sobrinos's wail resonated with each of them.

Argus's sword was drawn and he was scuttling towards the attackers as soon as Sobrinos fell. He could hear his cousin screaming, and Karine, and Astrid from her iron cell. The words were garbled in his ears.

His weapon cut through fabric and skin. Like a deranged painter without any sense for the craft, Argus daubed death with unmeasured strokes. Blood spewed and dripped in puddles, splattered against walls. The insides of the men were spilt, slaughtered like pigs. He was without remorse.

Argus did not question why these men were not wearing armor like the other guards, or why their weapons were of lesser quality. The sellsword could not focus on the faces of his enemy as he cut through them. He could only see red, and shadows, and death. It did not matter if they had families and friends; he did not care whether or not these men were only doing what they were paid to do. He was a fighter, a gladiator, and a sellsword.

Haakan Madrin.

Argus Gunther, even with another name, was the bastard child of a noble man, thrown away by his own mother and abandoned by his father. The world would know his pain.

"Stop!" Sobrinos shouted. Argus could not tell how many times the man had said the word. "They are dead. They are all dead."

Karine dropped a sword to the pile of dead bodies littering the hallway. There were a dozen or more.

Argus had not a clue that the female gladiator had joined the fight. She was lucky he had not cut her down as well.

"But who are they?" Karine asked.

Sobrinos held himself against the wall with one hand. His other shakily clutched the bolt resting in his gut. "These are from the *Hand of Tear'n*. They are thieves."

Argus scowled. "I don't understand. Why are they here? Why did they attack us?"

"Oh no," Sobrinos said. His eyes rested on one of the dead bodies. "That is Jebodiah Ekdal, Syomin Ekdal's little brother."

Argus hit the iron wall with a fist, his fingers

cracking from the impact.

The sound was deafened by the chiming of clinking armor. It sounded like an army of guards rushing in the corridor.

"We have to leave." Karine said. "We cannot fight the entire *Ward*."

Sobrinos concurred, hobbling towards the way they had come. Karine threw his arm over her shoulder to help him along. She avoided looking at the body of Abdul who lay among the throng of dead thieves.

Astrid's alarmed voice ascended. "Mr. Gunther."

Argus convulsed, chest rigid. His feet grew heavier with each step towards the noble lass's prison door. His hand came close to the cold surface and froze.

The sellsword could barely speak. "I will come back for you. I promise."

Chapter 11

Argus ignored the muffled yell and jerked the bloodied bolt from Sobrinos's stomach. His cousin caught a scream in his throat, pressing the gray cloth against the visible wound. Argus eyed the blood seeping through the white shirt to his belt line.

"Hold tighter and quit whining," Argus said gravelly, hunkering down in the back office of the *Bracken and Pine*. He pushed Sobrinos back into the wooden chair with a firm hand, and tossed the bolt to the ground. "You aren't dead yet."

In the doorway behind Argus, a gray-haired man, Tolliver Wolfram, hugged his sister, the gladiator, Karine the Swift. "Without healing magic, he will likely die," he said.

Argus turned his hooked nose toward the older man and glared.

Karine let go of her brother and said, "Listen to Tolliver. The Capsa Guard are known to lace their bolts with poison, and even if it were not so, he could very well die from infection."

"I...am..." Sobrinos tried, heaving with his hands clasped against his stomach. "I am aware...of the dangers. I knew the risk before we came to retrieve you from that cell, Karine."

"A gesture I would gladly repay, Lord Bloch," said Karine, shifting her light feet.

"No reason to make anymore promises," Tolliver said. "Abdul is dead and the debts have been paid. His body left at the scene will surely be traced back to the *Bracken and Pine*. There isn't a man, woman, or child in Hawkhurst who doesn't know Abdul worked under my directive." He slid his fingers through his thinning hair. "There is no other option. Karine and I must flee Hawkhurst tonight, whether through the front gate or into the Underverse, but we cannot stay here."

"Tolliver?" Karine raised her voice.

"No." Her brother deflected her questioning inflection. "We have not gone to this trouble only to be burned in the Skyway."

Argus grunted, standing from his kneeled position to face the man who had been managing the *Bracken and Pine* in the absence of the true owner, Link Sangrey.

"What trouble have you gone to?" Argus challenged. "You withheld information for your own interest. Abdul is dead and Sobrinos is injured. You did little more than sit in your warehouse and watch the clock tick."

"Abdul was my man, not yours," Tolliver responded curtly.

Argus tensed. In the past hour, he had slaughtered a dozen or more thieves, including the youngest brother of his ally, Syomin Ekdal, and that did not include the guardsmen standing watch in the *Ward*. He was not in the mood to be tested. One more death wouldn't add any additional weight to his conscious.

Karine, a gladiator like he had once been, stole the sneer from his face. "Abdul had every reason to rescue me from the *Ward*, but what of you two? Surely, there is something you wanted in exchange?"

Argus nodded, and expectantly turned to Tolliver.

"Abdul is dead," Tolliver said with absolution. "I owe you nothing."

Karine stepped in front of her brother, gripping his jacket before Argus could think of trying to intimidate the old man with his weapon. "Be wise, Tolliver."

"You do not know this man, Karine," said her brother, glaring at Argus over her shoulder. "My agreement was with the woman who travelled with him."

"And she is locked away in the *Ward*," Argus chimed, trembling at the thought. He could not save Astrid Lancaster, the noble from Galoroth, who he had first brought to Hawkhurst as a ransom. Now, she was ensnared in his plight, under the whim of Lord Jimi Oenus. The web he had been woven into was too complex to think about without profusely sweating.

Tolliver continued, "He has done horrendous things here in Hawkhurst, and deserves nothing from its people."

Karine the Swift retorted without pause, "The same can be said of any in Hawkhurst, including the both of us. Forget your pride, Tolliver. This man has given me freedom, and if it is in your power, you will give him whatever he wishes."

"We aren't free yet," Tolliver muttered.

She let go of his jacket. "We are closer than we have ever been."

Tolliver scrunched his brow, narrowing his eyes at Argus. The older man rocked back on his feet, finally shifting his eyes away. "Fine."

Argus took the opportunity, reiterating the purpose of their arrangement. "Tell me who asked you to scribe the letter to Jimi Oenus. Who sent the letter to House Oenus with the severed finger?"

"You mean Lillian Oenus's finger?"

"No, I don't," Argus said matter-of-factly, nostrils flaring. "I know the finger did not come from her hand, unless she regrows parts."

"You saw her?" Sobrinos exhaled noisily, before sucking in another breath. "Why did you not say something about looking for Lilian Oenus?"

Argus dipped his head in acknowledgement without facing his cousin. "It hadn't come up yet."

Sobrinos coughed.

Tolliver paused, considering Argus. "Syomin Ekdal requested the letter be scribed under the—"

Argus interjected, "I have spoken with Syomin, and he said he did not request the letter. He said the *Hand of Tear'n* were not directly involved."

"Where did you see Lillian? Was she in the company of Lord Ekdal?" Tolliver laughed with the obvious truth. Argus felt the blood drain from his face, his heart quickening. "Syomin had asked the letter to be completed for Lord Garnoc Hedlund. The thief is playing on words."

Sobrinos found the strength to speak again. "Why would the *Hunter's Guild* get involved?"

"The *Hunter's Guild* did attack me when I first came into Hawkhurst," Argus said.

Sobrinos grunted, holding his gut. "Lord Hedlund

is the brother of Lord Oenus's wife. Armine would be devastated to know her brother had anything to do with the kidnapping of her daughter."

"In the *Eadfel*, anything is possible." Tolliver shrugged. "And, I am not in the business of questioning motives or action. I am paid for a service and I provide the service. Truthfully, I do not know why this has brought *Haakan Madrin*," he sniffed at Argus disdainfully, "back to Hawkhurst, nor do I care."

Argus winced upon hearing his true name being said aloud by the warehouse manager. He had told Tolliver repeatedly to call him *Argus* and not *Haakan*.

"How noble of you," Sobrinos scoffed, laying his head back.

"Unless…" Argus rubbed his finger and thumb against each other, "Unless Armine is involved in the scheme herself."

"What?" Sobrinos gasped with his head half-cocked, having no strength to sit up straight. "What nonsense are you spitting?"

Argus winced. "Lillian is not being held against her will. She acted as though she were with Syomin of her own accord, but I had the sense there might be more to the story. I wonder if her mother convinced her to *disappear*."

"You think Lillian faked her own kidnapping? Whatever for?" Sobrinos contended. "Besides, Jimi and Armine have been married for years. Five children. The Oenus House has long been prosperous, and Jimi will soon extend into Upper City, where Armine will live a grandeur life than what she already does."

"Maybe so, but," Argus said, stretching his

memory to what he knew of Hawkhurst and its noble families. "Armine is foremost a Hedlund?"

Sobrinos's gaped with recognition. "Yes. A Hedlund!"

"Garnoc's sister." Argus nodded. "What does Garnoc have to gain by kidnapping Lillian? What do the Hedlunds gain?"

"Do you still have the letter?" Sobrinos asked.

Argus retrieved the letter from his inner pocket and handed it to his cousin.

Sobrinos grunted, scanning the words, and quickly said, "There is your answer." He dipped his head at Tolliver. "This letter was forged to appear in the hand of Lord Aaron Quist, Jimi's closest ally. They are trying to break apart the alliance, which will keep House Hedlund in their position after House Oenus moves to Upper City."

Argus sank back awestruck. "I may have unknowingly fed this lie by pointing the finger at House Quist myself before knowing better."

"So what?" Tolliver said. "You'd very well be better off to play along with the lie. The truth will not bring you any reward." Tolliver snorted with a shake of his head. "You think Lord Oenus will believe his wife and daughter are scheming against him? No. It is more likely you will be killed for even suggesting such a thing."

"He's right," Sobrinos said softly, coughing suddenly.

"Maybe not…" Argus wondered.

Sobrinos said, "Take me to my mother, Haakan. House Bloch will care for me."

Argus snapped his head toward his cousin. "Are

you mad? Do you understand what is at stake if I drop you off at the doorstep of my father's sister?"

"And what if you do not? Do you plan to hire a mage from the Ascension to heal me or...will you let me die?" Sobrinos indicted weakly.

Argus balled up his fists. "No. I will take you."

Chapter 12

Argus held Sobrinos's wrist firmly over his neck and shoulder, half dragging the man through the back alleyway of the *Bracken and Pine*. He could hear the rustling of guards moving up and down the streets, whether on patrol or in pursuit, he could not tell.

Sobrinos subdued a groan, turning his head into Argus's shoulder. His cousin clutched his stomach, balancing on one leg as though he were trying to lessen the pain.

"Stay with me," Argus said. Shadows flooded by the alleyway as the Capsa guard rushed by them. Argus raised his arm to keep Sobrinos still. "They must be looking for us," he said when they were out of earshot."

"They probably don't know what they are looking for." Sobrinos huffed, clenching his fist around Argus's wrist. "The *Ward* is a bloody mess of thieves and guards all strung together. At most, because of Abdul's body, they are looking for Karine and Tolliver."

Argus scowled. "Then, let's hope they are already on their way out of Hawkhurst. You know Tolliver would give up our names in an instant if he thought it'd benefit him."

Sobrinos nodded. "You are likely right. So, get me home before we are found."

With a low growl, Argus shuffled along the edge of the building and onto the cobblestone street, wary of any guardsman.

The trek to Sobrinos's estate from the *Bracken and Pine* was uneventful. The two did their best to blend into the evening roamers without drawing attention, plodding through the streets. In Hawkhurst, Argus assumed spies from noble houses were always watching, but he could not waste the time to worry about what he could not control.

Soon, Argus slugged up the stairway to the iron door, carrying his cousin in one hand and pushing the door open with his other.

"Mother," Sobrinos called out, collapsing to a knee more dramatically than Argus thought to be necessary.

A woman with a braided blonde knot hanging past her shoulders bolted into the foyer. The wrinkles under her eyes and at the edge of her lips were the only indicator of her age. "Sobrinos? What has happened?"

Sobrinos pulled his hand from his stomach for only a moment to reveal the split wound from the arrow. Blood oozed.

His mother, Lady Sophia Bloch, turned cold eyes to Argus. "Haakan? We thought you were dead! What have you done to my son?" Her voice was anything but calculated, piercing through the large home, and echoing off the rafters.

Argus snorted, squinting an eye at the woman, his father's sister. Every other person he interacted with noticed him at first sight. He was certain his scalp had a thin layer of hair, but his disguise was supposed to keep his identity hidden. "He is going to need magic if you want him to live…"

"He did not do this, mother," Sobrinos wheezed. "I brought this on myself, I assure you."

Sophia's eyes did not leave Argus. "Stop trying to protect him, Sobrinos. No one would believe you to be so stupid."

"What is going on here?" a heavy voice fell into the entryway, as a man—larger than Argus—stomped down the stairs. His hair was longer than his wife's, gray and black, with a stringy beard reaching his chest.

Sath Bloch may have been the lowest recognized Lord in Middle City, but he carried himself with as much authority as King Moors.

"Haakan nearly killed your son!" Sophia glared at Argus, and then turned to her husband reaching the bottom of the stairs. "Take the bastard to his father, or better yet, to his uncle."

Sath matched his wife's intensity, dropping his chin to gaze at Argus. He ignored his writhing son on the ground. "Cauthe-dammit, Haakan. What are you doing in Hawkhurst?"

"Trying to leave," Argus said, matching the gaze with equal authority. His eyes fell to his cousin, paling from loss of blood. "Sobrinos was trying to help, but the webs of the *Eadfel* are thick."

Almost knowingly, Sath nodded. "Does Rotrderd know you are here? Veina?"

The sound of his parents' names triggered his real name to resound in his head. Argus shook the sound out of his ears, reminding himself that his mother was still alive after his attempt to murder her when he last escaped Hawkhurst.

"No," Argus finally said. "They do not know I have come. I was not supposed to be here but a couple of hours."

"I think it best you tell me all you know," Sath said.

"What of your son?" Sophia asked with disdain.

Sath pulled at his beard, taking only a moment before responding. "Send for Thorin Awklee, the messenger boy for the House Etha."

Argus opened his mouth to protest, remembering the lad from the *Bracken and Pine* when he first arrived at Hawkhurst. He had avoided the boy, knowing the strength of the alliance between House Madrin and House Etha. If Thorin knew of his real name, his father would know of his presence within an hour.

His uncle, standing in front of him, grunted as if he knew Argus's worry. "The Ethas and Madrins both have a strong alliance with House Erixx in upper city. Thorin will be able to fetch a mage to heal Sobrinos."

"Why would House Erixx help you?" Argus growled.

"Because of our union with House Sybaris. Austris Erixx would do anything to help Uschi Sybaris, and her kin, which we are," Sath said matter-of-factly.

Argus groaned, seeing Sophia shuffle from the room to send a servant for Thorin. "Not only will you alert my father's house, but also my mother's. You are going to get me killed."

Sath huffed, "Haakan, you should have been dead a long, long time ago. I am beginning to think you will never die. Besides, from the look of things, you know less than you think you know. Now…why don't you tell me what all this is about?"

Argus pressed his mustache to his beard with confusion, but finally assented, settling in the sitting room with his uncle. Over the next several hours, he told his story. He shared his life beyond Hawkhurst, living with his Uncle Peter in Hawe and pursuing a career as a sellsword. Argus then told of his dealings with Landon Kern, his employer, who had betrayed him, placing him in the service of Jimi Oenus.

"Jimi does not know who I am, Sath," Argus said, rubbing his fingers together with agitation. "He believes I am Argus Gunther from Hawe, a simple sellsword sent here to settle his debt with Mr. Kern. He tells me that he will grant my freedom if I find those responsible for kidnapping his daughter."

Sath pulled his shoulders back, staring expectantly at Argus. "And?"

Argus twisted his hand into a fist at his side. "And I suspect Lillian Oenus kidnapped herself at the behest of her mother."

"House Oenus is divided?" Sath leaned back to study the ceiling in thought.

"Do not start playing the *Eadfel* with me," Argus growled. "I want out of this blasted city. I have no interest in furthering your House or any other."

"But you will not leave Hawkhurst without Lady Lancaster?" His uncle poked at him like a charred log in the fire. "It is unlike you to wait around. Why is she so special?"

Argus grimaced, turning his head away. Astrid Lancaster believed he had some good in him, or at least, she had suggested as much. He could not say anyone had ever said as much about him. "I don't know," he lied. "But she is in Hawkhurst because of me. I suspect I have an obligation to rescue her from *The Ward*."

"Your sense of honor, or whatever it is, will be used against you," Sath said.

Argus twisted his gaze back to his uncle. "You are going to use it against me." He said his words with such assurance, knowing the statement held more weight than a warning. "Why?"

"House Bloch hasn't held a deserving position in many years, Haakan," Sath said, "and frankly, I have you by the balls. Best you be manhandled by family than by some ruffian in the streets."

Argus instinctually grunted, scooting his hips further back on the couch. "Just tell me, what are you proposing?"

Sath stood from the chair. "You will tell Jimi of his wife's and daughter's treachery, and I will free your dear girl from the *Ward*."

"Jimi might have me killed for suggesting such a thing, whether he believes me or not," Argus said.

His uncle nodded. "With his ascension to Upper City on the table, I doubt Jimi will be murdering anyone, especially a Madrin. House Madrin is very close to having supreme power in Middle City. House Bloch will quickly gain power behind House Etha, if we play our cards right."

"He doesn't know I am a Madrin," Argus argued.

Sath blew air from his nostrils with amusement. "I don't think your beard is fooling anyone. Even if he does string you up, Astrid Lancaster will be free. I assure you."

A banging from the front door echoed.

Lady Sophia dashed across the opening of the foyer, barely in sight from the sitting room where Argus and Sath sat. Hushed voices mumbled opposite side of the wall. Seconds later, Sophia zipped back up the staircase where Sobrinos had been taken to rest. Behind her followed an old man with a white beard, shrouded in a black robe.

Behind them followed Thorin Awklee, the courier to House Etha. The dark haired boy from the *Bracken and Pine* caught Argus's gaze as he passed the doorway, a sliver of a smile forming up to his cheekbones.

Heavy footsteps bounded up the stairs, and then the door slammed shut. Another set resonated from the foyer. Argus swallowed as a third man stepped into the doorway to face him and Sath.

"Rotrderd," his uncle acknowledged, dipping his head to the more noble of the two men. "I thought you might come."

Argus's father unfastened his blue cloak, embedded with the red spiral circles of House Madrin, letting it fall to the floor. He peered down his crooked nose at Argus. "I had to see it for myself."

Forcing himself to his feet, Argus coldly regarded Rotrderd. The hair atop his father's head was no longer than the red hair prickling his father's chin and upper lip.

"There are no pit walls—no Arena—to separate us here, Rotrderd," Argus said, sneering. "You should have brought your guardsmen," he gazed to his father's naked belt, "or, at least, your sword."

His uncle moved to intercept them. "Keep your head, Haakan."

"My name is not Haakan," Argus snarled.

Rotrderd spoke steadily over Sath, "Let *Haakan* say what he will."

"I have forgotten that name. I am a bastard—not a person in Hawkhurst doesn't know it. You dumped me," he retorted, moving his hand to the sword at his side.

"No," Rotrderd said with enough calm to ease a widow's suffering. "You are a bastard because you attacked Veina—your own mother, while she sat helpless in her home—after running away from the Arena. And then, you deserted Hawkhurst like some dishonorable coward. Why my brother gave you shelter in Hawe, I will never understand. Mercy was the last thing you deserved."

"Veina could have kept me in House Sybaris. You could have taken me into your home. Instead, I was thrown to the gladiator pits," Argus fumed. "I was only five."

"Your mother kept you safe until then, did she not?" Rotrderd's face hardened.

"Is that supposed to make me feel better?" asked Argus. He gripped the hilt of his weapon until his knuckles ached. "Show me love until I'm old enough to understand it, and then forsake me!" He pulled the weapon from its sheathe, hearing the familiar cling of metal against metal. "I killed hundreds in those pits, and each one had your face."

"I came to every fight you fought."

"To elevate your station in Middle City. To increase your wealth. You took away my freedom!"

Rotrderd frowned, and grunted. "The gladiators were meant to make you stronger before you joined me in our House, Haakan. Your recklessness cost you your freedom, not me."

"Put your sword down, Haakan," Sath said, scooting closer to him, "or your haste will cost you more than liberty. I told you that you don't know everything."

"I have nothing left to lose," Argus rumbled. "Once the Capsa Guard find me, I'll be sent to the Skyway. I am a fugitive from the Arena."

"You were a free gladiator, Haakan," Rotrderd said, raising an eyebrow. "You could have left anytime you wanted…"

"What?" Argus's knees weakened. "You told me I had been enslaved…I…" He searched for the right words.

His father stood fast, etched from stone.

"I nearly killed Veina..."

"But you didn't," Sath said. "She is not dead. If men were arrested in Hawkhurst for trying to kill a noble, there would not be any men left."

"Just tonight, I slaughtered men at *The Ward*." Argus felt himself fighting to find some injustice he had caused, worthy of punishment.

"And, who knows about your involvement? Who here would tell?" Sath offered, lifting an eyebrow under his bushy bangs.

Argus dropped his arm to his side, reluctant to let loose of the blade. His father tensed his jaw, and continued.

"This is the *Eadfel*, Haakan. This is how things in Hawkhurst are done. House Madrin is strong because we carve our own futures, and are not subdued by the threat of sorrow. To be a Madrin, you have to understand there is purpose in our misery." His father folded his arms across his chest. "I could not teach you what you needed to know as a father. You had to be molded by hardship. You had to learn that our suffering teaches us better than any oration."

He could only stare at Rotrderd, uncertain as to whether he could believe the man, let alone trust him.

"The question is whether or not you have learned what was required?" Rotrderd added shrewdly.

Argus's body went weak. The sword slipped from his fingers, clanging to the ground. His mind tangled with confusion. Years of hate and frustration washed away.

Haakan Madrin.

He conceded. "I have."

Chapter 13

Creon's Inn had been buzzing the last day with whispers of the happenings at *The Ward*, and the disappearance of Tolliver Wolfram. Rumor was the stand-in owner of the *Bracken and Pine* had fled to the Underverse with his sister, and Link Sangrey—the true proprietor—was in route to return. Argus had evaded most of the chitter-chatter, remaining in his small room upstairs.

His father and uncle had said to stay out of sight until Lord Jimi Oenus sent for him. Argus was certain it would not be long. After a day and a half, he was already growing anxious for the inevitable meeting.

He pulled the sharp razor along his scalp, scraping away the small red strands, and then rinsed off the blade in the water bowl. Argus caught sight of his long, red beard in the small mirror leaning against the dresser. He tugged at the curled hair gently, fixating his gaze on his hooked nose, the passed-down trait of his father.

No doubt, Rotrderd was an intelligent man, managing the affairs of House Madrin for the past many years. He had suggested the other night that

Argus would rejoin House Madrin as his legitimate eldest son, inheriting the estate and ultimately the title of Lord. Argus wanted to believe his father told the truth, but this was the same man who had left him with the gladiators as a child. If Rotrderd would go to such lengths to play the *Eadfel*, who knew what other tricks he might have kept hidden.

"Did you kill my brother, Haakan?" the familiar, cracked voice spoke mellifluously.

Argus almost jumped, startled by the sudden sound in what he had thought to be an empty room. He looked into the mirror to see Syomin Ekdal, crouching in the corner. Argus had no explanation for how the man had snuck into his room without being heard.

The owner, Creon Nass, would have brought him up personally if the thief had been welcomed. Argus could not help but wonder how long Syomin had been waiting, whether he had just arrived or had been in hiding—maybe under the bed—for hours.

Syomin's long black, braided locks dipped on either side of his shadowed face as he aimed a hand crossbow at Argus's back.

Argus hid his concern, skating the razor along his scalp again before dowsing it in the water again. He looked at the bolt of the weapon for a second before focusing back on his shaving.

"Answer me," Syomin hissed. "Did you cut down Jebodiah when he was sent to get the two women *you* asked me to retrieve?"

His jaw tensed in sudden remembrance. He had forgotten the full of the conversation he had with Syomin and Lillian at the *Hand of Tear'n*. He had agreed to lead Lord Oenus to believe House Quist was responsible for Lillian's disappearance, if Syomin freed Astrid and Karine.

He had never thought Syomin would have followed through with the task. Yet, all this time, he had been asking himself why the *Hand of Tear'n* had been at *The Ward*.

Argus could only guess how corrupt the situation appeared. He had asked Syomin to send men, and then killed them.

He searched for the right words. "I heard…" Argus turned to face the master thief, his old employer. "I heard about Jebodiah last night, like most of Hawkhurst. I didn't—"

"Do not lie to me, Haakan. My men saw you leave *The Ward* after the brawl. I know your way in battle, and my men were slaughtered without shame. Hacked into pieces. You really think I'd believe a few Capsa guards would leave such a bloodbath." Syomin sneered, rising to his feet in the corner. "Armine had said you told Lord Oenus that House Quist was behind Lillian's kidnapping. You had done what you promised, and I did as I swore to do."

Argus's mind swirled, faintly remembering the uncomfortable conversation with Jimi Oenus in his study days ago. His wife, Armine, had intruded for only a moment before disappearing, or so he had thought. The information confirmed what Argus had already considered. Armine was in league with destroying her husband's rise to power.

He was not sure he cared to know the details anymore.

Argus realized Syomin kept on, "I helped you escape Hawkhurst once, and I have been doing everything in my power to help you once more. So, why did you kill my brother?"

Haakan Madrin.

The voice in his head came from nowhere, causing his ears to ring. His father's words followed. *You were a free gladiator. You could have left anytime you wanted.* Argus gulped, lifting his eyes to Syomin with as much innocence as he could muster. He suddenly realized Syomin had never done anything for him except promise what freedom Argus already had.

He hated to do what had to be done, but as his Uncle Peter said, *'if you do not want a man to learn the truth, don't allow him to learn'.*

He could not hide that he had killed Jebodiah Ekdal forever. The truth would eventually come out.

"House Ekdal owns the Arena. Why did you never tell me I was free? You knew the whole time, did you not?" asked Argus, calling Syomin's bluff. Some questions were best asked with questions.

He had to clench his fist to keep his hand steady.

Argus watched the lump in Syomin's throat bulge as the man swallowed hard. "What are you talking about?" he replied shakily. The hand crossbow fell sideways by a hair, and Syomin quickly repositioned it to point at Argus's chest.

His Uncle Peter had told him after coming to Hawe, *'The nature of snow is to be cold. It stays true to itself. Be snow, Haakan. Be snow.'*

Argus swelled his chest, and cleared his throat. "I could have left the pits, Lower City, or even Hawkhurst whenever I wanted, but you kept me bound to the Arena, fighting for you. I made sacrifices to you, Maggie, and Cauthe knows who else to secure my freedom. You always told me that Rotrderd capitalized off my fights. How much did you make? What did you have to gain?"

"You killed my brother because you think I used you?" Syomin's jaw asked, eyes flashing.

"I did not say I killed your brother," Argus remarked, gripping the handle of the razor blade in his fist.

His words were unheard as Syomin raised his voice in anger. "Every single piece of wasted human flesh is used in this damned city. Naturally, I used you. Your father used you. Your mother used you. Your friends used you. You were born to be used by others. That is your lot in life, you worthless, pathetic dog. And I gained everything!"

Pushing away his thoughts, Argus thundered forward, slanting his body as he propelled himself at Syomin. The bolt from the hand crossbow zinged by him, harmlessly, piercing into the dresser drawer behind him. Argus smiled as fear skirted over Syomin's face, and then sunk his knee into the man's stomach. The master thief winced in anguish, having little hope to compete against the former gladiator in hand-to-hand combat.

In a fluid movement, he knocked Syomin back into the corner with a hard-pressed fist to the man's cleft chin. A second fist soon followed, hammering down on the thief's skull. Syomin crashed into the boards, the air audibly leaving his lungs, and a distorted groan fleeing his lips. He sank to his knees.

He puffed. "Haa-kan. Wait."

"We are done talking, Syomin," Argus said, grabbing the man by his black cloak. He clenched the razor in his free hand, pressing it against the master thief's jugular.

Syomin gaped back at him, frantically, his hands scaling up through the space between them to hold back Argus's hand. The man's eyes were widespread, his tongue hanging from his throat, looking for the right words to—

Argus slashed his throat, ignored the blood splattering across his hands, and dropped Syomin to the floor. The thief gurgled with tremulous lips until he was dead.

Stepping back, Argus watched the crimson liquid puddle against the wooden floorboards.

The door swung open behind him, and he heard the gruff sound of Creon Nass, the self-proclaimed, free gladiator. "What have you done, Mr. Gunther?" There was a brief pause before the innkeeper answered his own question. "You killed Syomin Ekdal. Do you know who that is? Lord Oenus will send you to the Skyway for this or worse. I warned you that there were worse things than death."

Argus hummed under his breath, eyes locked on the dead body of the man he once thought a friend. "You do not know everything, Creon. Go ahead. Take me to Lord Oenus."

Chapter 14

The master-crafted lute on the back of Lord Oenus kept Argus's attention. The blonde-haired man meandered around the fanciful desk in his study, scowling with the intensity of any gladiator in the Arena. Argus kept his feet pressed to the floorboards, grounding himself, trying to ignore Creon's firm grip on his shoulder. Instead, he focused on keeping his nose tense and his breath even. The last thing he needed was for Lord Oenus to recognize his Madrin bloodline.

Jimi rapped his fingers on the chiseled, sapphire desk. The yellow light inside glimmered, bouncing off of the inner gemstone.

"It's true, Lord Oenus," Creon said. "I have a dead Ekdal sprawled out in his room. The bastard slit his throat and left him to bleed out."

Argus winced. If things went the way his father promised, he would no longer be called a *bastard*.

Jimi took a breath, pulling his hand away from the desk. "And then he asked to see me?"

"That's right, my Lord," Creon said.

"Mr. Gunther," Jimi said with a clear sense of

disdain, "you were hired to pay off Mr. Kern's debt to me. Surely, you understand that your actions reflect directly on my House."

Argus dipped his chin, making eye contact with Lord Oenus. He shifted ever so slightly in his cushioned seat. "I do."

"Do you want to die?" Jimi asked.

"Not today," Argus answered.

"Then why did you murder, Syomin Ekdal?" Lord Oenus unstrapped his lute, gripping it in his hand.

"For justice," Argus said unflinching, "and to protect your reputation."

"Protect me?" Jimi clicked his tongue, nodding to Creon, who tightened his grip. The Lord stepped closer, leaning in with a scowl. "This is not the time to be playing games. Explain yourself."

Argus grimaced under the strength of the gladiator behind him. "I discovered Lord Ekdal was directly connected to the disappearance of your daughter."

"Lilly?" Jimi interrupted with surprise, stooping back. His gaze softened.

Argus cleared his throat, nodding. "Syomin knew I had him figured out, and he tried to stop me from telling you. You will find that he was armed with a crossbow, and a bolt is lodged in the dresser in my room." Argus rubbed his fingers together to remain unruffled, holding to the partial lie. "Lucky for me, he is better at thieving than firing bolts."

Lord Oenus's blue eyes flashed, looking to Creon for an explanation.

"There have been no rumors in the inn to suggest the thieves are involved in Lillian's kidnapping, Lord Oenus," Creon said. "Outside of Jebodiah and a handful of the bandits raiding *The Ward* last night—for whatever reason—most would say they have been quieter than usual."

"Lord Capsa said there was more than thieves in his complex last night," Jimi stated, considering Argus again. After a moment, he added, "What of the bolt and crossbow?"

Argus heard the floor creak behind him as the large innkeeper shifted his weight. "There is a crossbow near Syomin's body and a bolt in the dresser."

Jimi paused as though he were trying to choose his words, or considering whether or not there could be another explanation. Finally, he redirected focus by saying, "Last we spoke, Mr. Gunther, you placed blame on House Quist for Lilly's disappearance. I spoke to Aaron—"

"I know this to no longer be true," Argus assured, lifting his chin. "Lord Aaron Quist has nothing to do with Lillian, and neither does his son, Frederick. They are innocent."

"Indeed." Jimi cleared his throat, carefully surveying Argus. "You have clearly found your place in Hawkhurst, and have learned its mannerisms. Why don't you stop speaking in riddles, and tell me what you do know to be true? Tell me, where is my daughter?"

"I first need some assurances, my Lord," Argus said, growing bolder. Jimi provided a questioning look. Argus continued, "First off, I have a dead man in my room, and I am afraid the news regarding your daughter is not what you would expect. I don't want to be facing repercussions for my honesty."

"Honesty is all I have asked for since our crossing,

and I must say, you do not have the reputation of being an honest man. In any case, you are not in a position to be making demands," Jimi said, pulling his instrument to his torso, and running his fingers across the strings of the lute. Argus felt his head grow light and the room began to vibrate. "Believe me, *Haakan*, I can get information from you whether you want to share it or not. I have the power to make you an honest man."

Haakan Madrin.

His chest momentarily tightened. The fact that Lord Oenus knew his name washed over him in a moment of panic. Yet he could not find the means to respond.

Argus sensed his eyelids growing heavy as Creon's grip loosened for the first time since leaving the inn. A jolt of energy surged from temple to temple making him shudder. The enchantment intensified as Jimi began to hum his lullaby.

Argus's skin prickled and his legs numbed.

And then a crash sounded behind Argus, jerking him from the spell. He twisted half-dazed to find Creon collapsed and snoring on the ground.

"Cauthe-dammit, Creon," Jimi muttered, uneasily shifting forward.

Argus desperately took his chance, holding his head to steady his senses. "Listen, Armine was the one who did it. She and Lillian conspired against you, Lord Oenus. I am not your enemy."

The lute swung downward by the neck in Jimi's hand, nearly connecting with the floor of the foyer. He tensed his jaw. "What did you say?"

Argus gripped his head, shaking away the fuzzy feeling that swarmed. "Your wife and Lillian planned this madness. It was all a ruse."

"It cannot be." The Lord shook his head. "You are lying."

"I saw Lillian with Lord Ekdal," Argus said. "She is fine. Never the better. She said she wanted you to think House Quist had taken her, to destroy your alliance. Lillian said she was in love with another man."

"Who?" he demanded.

"She never said, my Lord. But your wife and daughter plot against you all the same," Argus said.

"You are playing the *Eadfel*. You are Haakan Madrin. I cannot trust you," Lord Oenus stated with disbelief, his knuckles white around the neck of the instrument.

Argus eyed the lute, knowing Jimi must have used it last time they had been in this room to learn of his real identity. There was no hiding his bloodline any longer.

"Yes, I am Haakan Madrin. But I am not playing the *Eadfel*," Argus disputed. "I hate the *Eadfel*. I want no part of it. I told you I wanted to go home. You said finding your daughter would allow me to leave this cursed city. And I found her…at the *Hand of Tear'n*."

"To Hawe, *Haakan*," Jimi said mockingly. "Is that your home?"

Argus swelled his chest. "Yes. Hawe has been more a home to me than Hawkhurst ever was. I will return to my uncle's house."

"It would be unwise for you to do anything else than leave Hawkhurst given the chance. No matter what you hear, you would not be welcome among most company—even those who would call themselves family," Jimi said.

"What do you mean?" Argus asked, doing his best to seem aloof to the possibility.

"Best you trust my judgment, Haakan." Jimi studied Argus. He moved a strand of hair from his cheek, saying, "And what of Mr. Kern?"

"I have nothing left to do with Kern, my Lord," Argus said, thinking of Lord Oenus's words about his family. Jimi may very well be trying to frighten him into leaving Hawkhurst. "The cheat is no longer my problem."

"Interesting how a short time in Hawkhurst puts things into perspective." Jimi hummed, peering at Argus, and then, as though he had made up his mind, he bobbed his head. "*Haakan*, you point the finger at my wife, but for what reason? Nothing you have said tells of her involvement. And you killed the only man who could be questioned to corroborate your story."

"The *Hunter's Guild* attacked me and Lady Lancaster after we arrived in Hawkhurst, when she was taken to the Ascension," Argus began. "Again, they were trying to stop us, but why? Lord Garnoc Hedlund leads them, and he is Armine's brother, right? Wouldn't he want to help find his niece? Why would he stop those you hired to discover Lillian's whereabouts instead of looking for her himself?"

Argus recognized the knowing look in Lord Oenus's eyes. It was the same expression he had found on the faces of countless opponents in the Arena before killing them.

Acceptance.

"Find Lord Hedlund and question him with your *lute*. Question your wife! I am telling you the truth.

They are trying to protect the Hedlund name, my Lord," Argus pressed, "by destroying you and House Quist. House Ekdal was their easy ally, finally finding the chance to ascend from Lower City."

"You almost sound like a noble, Haakan," Jimi said, watching him with a concentrated gaze. Lord Oenus set Argus at unease, especially with the man's continued compulsion to use his real name.

Creon stirred from behind Argus, groaning softly.

The sound of the front door creaking open, followed by the clicking of shoes stole Jimi's attention from Argus.

Argus turned his head to see Armine, her dark locks swaying and hands folded across her waist as she entered the study. Her eyes drifted to Creon, rousing himself on the floor, and then to her husband.

"Jimi," Armine said hesitantly, eyeing the lute in his hand, "what is going on in here?"

"Darling…" Jimi said with a wicked smile, strumming the instrument slowly. "Have a seat. We have so much to talk about."

Chapter 15

The blue cloak settled over Argus's shoulders lightly, swaying behind him as he walked toward the dining hall in his father's estate. The stairs leading to the second floor faded behind him, along with the room his father had placed him in to rest. He had heard countless promises of his lodgings, his riches, and his titles in the past twenty-four hours. Part of him could not believe this was really happening. He had been accepted into the Madrin family, and would be considered a Lord.

He felt a tightening in the pit of his stomach, much like when he used to battle in the Arena. This new venture would be unlike any fight he had ever faced before.

He looked down and traced his fingers along the red spiral circles, the sign of House Madrin, stitched into the fabric. Wearing the garment marked him as a noble among the Madrin family. No longer could he be denied his birthright. No longer would he be called a bastard.

His soft black boots were barely heard as he strolled along the carpeted path. The smell of roasted boar and baked bread consumed the manor. The rumble of chatter reached his ears, much like the thunderous sounds of patrons watching gladiators from the stands.

Argus entered the dining hall about the time that Rotrderd stood from the end of the table, raising his porcelain cup toward the hallway from which Argus emerged. "Friends and family, I present to you, Haakan Madrin, my eldest. He has finally returned to his home to take his rightful place here, in House Madrin." His father motioned to the empty chair next to him at the head of the extra-wide table. "Please, my son, pick up your glass and join me in a toast."

A second porcelain cup, filled to the brim with red wine, awaited for Argus.

A round of light applause resounded around the crowded table, intensifying the continued chattering among the guests. Argus scrunched his mustache to his beard, recognizing those who had been invited to his welcoming party.

Foremost, his father's other children, his half-siblings, gathered around the table. None of them were particularly known to him, outside of their names. The eldest male, a head of red hair to his shoulders, had his jaw clamped so tightly shut he may have been cracking his teeth. He stood near his father, glaring at the empty spot meant for Argus. His name was Glackorn, he thought.

The other siblings were younger, if only by a handful of years. Still, Argus could not mistake the glowers or avoided glances as they half-heartedly slapped their hands together.

Argus only made it two steps closer to his reserved

seat when Lord Sath Bloch grabbed his hand, shaking it with a firm grip. Argus gripped the man's hand with equal fervor, although startled. "Did you hear already about House Oenus? Private circles are shaming Jimi, and he has subsequently placed his wife and daughter on house arrest. Now, Upper City has rejected Jimi from ascending." His uncle slapped him on the shoulder with a wide grin separating his dark mustache from his long beard. "Not to mention House Hedlund has shrunk back with the *Hunter's Guild* acting out against a noble house. Listen, you have given House Madrin and House Bloch a stronger standing by revealing Armine's scheme, and deserve my personal thanks. I knew you had greatness in you. You played the *Eadfel* as well as Jimi does that lute, Haakan. Enjoy your moment. You deserve this."

Argus nodded, having difficulty finding a response. "Thank you," he mumbled. The roar of applause increased around the table after his simple words. Someone whistled. Another shouted his name.

"Where is Astrid?" Argus asked his uncle, elevating his voice to be heard.

Sath only grinned wider, tilting his hand down the line of folks along the table. Argus searched frantically, seeing the familiar blonde locks further ahead.

Argus passed by Sath's wife, Sophia. She remained facing the table ahead, not bothering to give Argus any attention as he passed. Next to her stood Sobrinos, who surprisingly grabbed him.

"We will have our own celebration after this is over, I promise you," he said with a grin. Argus gave a concerned look, eyeing Sobrinos. His cousin dipped his head, pausing only for a moment to smack his stomach nonchalantly. "Don't worry about me. I am fully healed and ready for our next adventure."

A hand smacked him on the back, urging him forward, when an unfamiliar man gripped his shoulder and stretched out his hand. "Vahka Etha. A pleasure to meet you, at last, Haakan." Argus's mind riddled, remembering the name from somewhere. He grasped the hand, and felt something pressed into his palm. The dark-haired man leaned inward and whispered, "A message from Maggie. Best to read it now."

And then, with a grin, the man leaned back with a laugh louder than the rest, turning back to his wooden chair. The mentioning of Madame Maggie Halum reminded Argus that this was the son of Lord Etha, who had a fascination with whores.

He twisted his palm to see the small parchment pressed into one hand. A single word was written: *Poison.*

Argus swallowed, glancing to his drink sitting near his father. He hardly had time to process the information before Astrid Lancaster, with her light hair shimmering, stepped out from the masses. Her blue eyes were tear-stained as she reached out to him for a hug.

Argus embraced her.

"Mr. Gunther, thank you," she sobbed, wrapping her arms around his neck. She buried her head into his chest. "Lord Bloch told me all you had done to rescue me."

Unsure of whether she spoke of Sath or Sobrinos, he simply held her sobbing body, forgetting the many who surrounded them. He whispered in her ear. "Are you alright? Were you hurt?"

She pulled back to look into his eyes, stopping for a moment to see the emblem on his cloak. "I will never touch magic again, but I am alive. That is something more than what I thought was possible. Tomorrow, I will head back to Galoroth to find my brother, and my father. I will not be coming back to Hawkhurst."

"Good," he stumbled with his words. "Hawkhurst is no place for a noble woman like yourself."

"You should come back with me," she said, almost pleadingly. "This place…you said it yourself…there is nothing here for you. Don't play their games," she warned.

She nervously bit her lip, he guessed to hold back more tears from flowing. The piece of parchment in his hand crumbled in his fist.

Argus glanced to the seat next to Rotrderd. His father reached for the wine sitting in front of Argus's seat and held it up expectantly.

"You know as well as any that the *Eadfel* is not something I like to play, but I have to see this through," Argus said. His father and uncle had used him to separate Glackorn from Lillian, and boost House Madrin to greater power while weakening House Oenus.

His eyes touched the emblem on his cloak once more. They would not accept him into the family. No, his father would kill him now that he had served his purpose.

Astrid closed her eyes. She mouthed the words, but Argus heard her anyway. "Hawkhurst only has death to offer."

"This is my family. My blood," he replied. "It

makes sense that my fate should be in their hands. There are worse things than death."

"It does not have to be so." Then, Astrid spoke familiar words that Argus had heard before from Jimi Oenus. "There is also family beyond blood."

He understood the meaning of the words. Family or otherwise, especially in Hawkhurst, had the potential to be dangerous.

Argus gripped her hand, saying, "I am not afraid to die. Go home, Lass. Don't wait for the morning. Just leave. I…I am staying here."

She opened her mouth once more as though she might say something, and then shut it abruptly and nodded. Dropping her chin, she walked by him to leave.

He did not bother to look back at Astrid, making his way to his father. Although his feet felt heavy as he neared the front of the table, he stood with determination, like a gladiator on the battlefield.

"Ladies and gentlemen, my son…" Rotrderd started. Argus held onto his cup, watching the red liquid inside swirl against the inside of the glass. His father digressed into telling the tale of Argus's deeds, speaking of his contribution to House Madrin. Though Argus only half heard. Instead, the insides of his cup stared back at him, speaking of its dire purpose.

The moment slowed.

The cups lifted around him with echoed shouts of exultation. He minded his father, next to him, who gulped from his glass. Argus's eyes scanned the room, eyes falling on Sobrinos, Sath, and Lady Sophia, who did the same. At the far end, he caught Astrid's blue eyes as she disappeared, exiting the far door to leave the residence.

Argus's gaze met the dark eyes of Lord Vahka Etha, who pushed his own cup away. At that time, Argus realized the full of the message.

Glackorn Madrin started coughing first, blood spewing from his lips, and grabbing his stomach. His hands helplessly traced up to his neck, and then the rest of the guests imitated his half-brother's desperate attempts to cling to life. Argus looked on in horror as his cousin, uncle, and aunt crumpled forward sucking air through bubbled blood oozing from their lips, like a fish suffocating from water.

Suddenly, Rotrderd grabbed Argus's arm, pulling at him. Argus stared into the man's reddened eyes. His father's neck convulsed, veins popping from under the skin. "Haa-kan," he wheezed, falling to the floor.

Argus dropped his cup. It shattered at his feet.

He stared at the litter of dead bodies surrounding the long table until finally resting on Lord Vahka Etha, untouched by the poison.

Vahka dipped his head with admiration. "Lord Oenus sends his regards for your sudden loss, Lord Madrin."

ABOUT THE AUTHOR

Joshua Robertson was born in Kingman, Kansas on May 23, 1984. A graduate of Norwich High School, Robertson attended Wichita State University where he received his Master's in Social Work with minors in Psychology and Sociology. His bestselling novel, *Melkorka*, the first of *The Kaelandur Series*, was released in 2015. Known most for his *Thrice Nine Legends Saga*, Robertson enjoys an ever-expanding and extremely loyal following of readers, counting R.A. Salvatore & J.R.R. Tolkien among his literary influences.

www.robertsonwrites.com

Printed in Great Britain
by Amazon